To Kim
from the author
Tetyana Conr.
12/12/201.

MW01121799

Love and Mystery

Love Through Art

Love and Mystery

Love Through Art

by Tetyana Conrad

Editor

Cheryl Martin

Kurt Conrad

Senior Publisher

Steven Lawrence Hill Sr.

Awarded Publishing House

ASA Publishing Company

A Publisher Trademark Title page

ASA Publishing Company
Awarded Best Publisher for Quality Books

105 E. Front St., Suite 203
Monroe, Michigan 48161
www.asapublishingcompany.com

Copyrights©2011 Tetyana Conrad, All Rights Reserved
Book: Love and Mystery *"Love Through Art"*
Date Published: 04.2011
Edition 1 *Trade Paperback*
Book ASAPCID: 2380568
ISBN: 978-0615479514
Library of Congress Cataloging-in-Publication Data

This book was published in the United States of America.
State of Michigan

A Publisher Trademark Title page

DEDICATIONS

For my granddaughter
>
> *Nika, my son Vladislav, his wife Inga, my sister Valeria, my brother Oleg and all my family in Eastern Europe.*

For my mother
>
> *Henrietta and in memory of my father, Grigory.*

For my husband
>
> *Kurt Conrad, who provided support and invaluable help re-wording and editing this book.*

For Mary Johnson
>
> *and all my family in America.*

PROLOGUE

America has been called the land of opportunity, and New York City has been at the center of that belief. Many people migrate to this city hoping that it changes their future. People come here to make their mark in business, economics, politics, art and music. Each settles the area of the city which caters to his or her talents and profession. Some fail, while others succeed. There are those who distinguish themselves because they have the talent to begin with and there are others whose talent is forged on a road of trial and error...learning from his or her mistakes. Their success can be in several ways - a meteoric rise to the top, or it might be achieved as the result of many failures. Some can also be born into wealth and success, while others come upon it by a stroke of sheer luck. They just might be at the right place at the right time.

However, something unexplainable can happen to a very select few. It catapults them into a world of dreams. They can enjoy the fruits of that world, but it just happened...it wasn't their intention. They just hoped and prayed for success, like all the others. For some, it can be like a nightmare, but for others, it can lead to something extraordinary.

Love and Mystery

Love Through Art

by Tetyana Conrad

CHAPTER 1

The SoHo district, in New York City, is an area of fabulous shopping, and an abundance of art galleries. A lot of younger artists from across the USA move here to achieve their goals and dreams. They set up studios and apartments in old cast iron buildings, which were once warehouses and factories. In one of these buildings, is a beautiful young woman named Nicole. She has long black hair, large brown eyes and a white face with peach colored cheeks. She is painting a picture in her apartment studio. Nicole is an abstractionist. She tried painting in other styles and methods, but found abstractionism to be her calling.

Nicole has painted a few pictures, putting her feelings and emotions in her painting. She has the idea that she might one day display her pictures in a gallery because she has enough talent. She dreams of her future and imagines a long hall adorned with beautiful abstract paintings. In the center of the gallery is a picture of a spiral with changing colors, red to orange to green to yellow. Inside the spiral there are two figures, a man and a woman. They are holding each other and flying. She returns to reality from her dream and begins to paint the same picture that was in her dream. As she is painting the picture, she had a vision in which she hears music, and sees the face of a young man with blue eyes.

Also, in one of these buildings, at the same time, a young man named Mike is composing and playing music in the studio in his apartment. He writes and sings about his feelings and emotions. He is a handsome young man of medium height, with dark hair and blue eyes. While he is composing, he has a vision of a young woman and paintings of many colors behind her. This vision gives him the energy to continue to compose music describing his feelings and emotions.

CHAPTER 2

Nicole is painting a picture in her studio, but it doesn't seem right. She is very depressed and doesn't know what she should do. She feels unlucky, because she has no money and no boyfriend. However, she does have a lot of friends who love her, enjoy being around her and give her good words and compliments. She thinks, *all the time my friends tell me that I'm nice looking, a very good person inside, that I'm smart and intelligent, friendly and always ready to help others and yet I feel so alone. My dream is to meet someone with whom I will feel completely whole.*

She returns to her painting and has the vision that she had earlier, in which she hears music and sees the face of a young man. The music she hears makes her forget about her depression and negative thoughts. Her heart and soul begin to fill with happiness and harmony. From this music she begins to paint. However, she is painting unusually fast. She is not thinking and her hand is moving like it is separate from her body. It's like she's in another dimension. After a while, she stops and thinks *where am I? And what's going on?*

The next moment she realizes that she is in the same

small studio in her apartment but everything is different. It is brighter and there are many pictures. She can't believe she did all this. It makes her feel very happy. In front of her is one of the pictures she painted. The more she looks at it, the more she loves it. But, there is something mysterious about this picture. When she looks at it, the energy that went into painting this picture returns to her. The energy moves around her and through her. It stops inside her, and she feels as if she gained some knowledge, some understanding of why she is here and why she is painting. She wishes to share her happiness with someone who will be close to her. He will be very understanding and supportive. She feels that she is on the road to big changes in her life and this makes her feel very excited and happy. Nicole looks around and sees all kinds of pictures for this small studio and all kinds of thoughts come to her mind. In particular, she asks herself, *what's next? What should I do now?* and she has the dream again. There is a long gallery adorned with many pictures on the walls that are signed by her. She is surrounded by a lot of people, and they are all very excited and giving her compliments. This makes her very happy. The whole scene is unbelievable. It is a very happy moment. It is like a dream come true.

CHAPTER 3

Mike, the young singer/songwriter, is sitting by his piano. He is just relaxing and thinking about nothing. All of a sudden he has a vision. He sees a beautiful girl, and pictures with bright colors behind her. Upon returning to reality, everything looks different. It is like he has returned from another world. All the colors seem brighter and he starts composing. While writing music, he has another vision. Mike sees many pictures of circles, ovals and rings which are behind the girl. These pictures are in different colors, white, red, green, yellow, purple, orange, gold and silver. The pictures give him creative energy. He forgot about everything else and just composed music.

This was like his big start. After this, whenever he had the vision of the girl and the pictures, he would compose music. It was as if he had been given a new life. This gave him great happiness and the feeling that his life would be getting better and better. He felt as if something very important and serious would be coming into his life. However, he was still just like a boy with a lot of friends with whom he had a lot of fun. He would party, go to bars, drink beer or wine and go dancing. He remembered that his best friend, Max was having a party tonight, and that he was invited. In this sense, he was just another person, just one of the guys. Mike was a childhood friend with whom Max grew up with.

Max was a well known divorce lawyer. He invited friends from the university he attended and friends with whom he grew up. It was a typical party. There was a lot of food, drinking, smoking and dancing. Most of the people who attended this party were single. One of the partygoers was a girl named Susan who attended the same university as Max and had graduated with a major in philosophy. There were many people sitting and listening to her with all of their attention. Mike decided to find out what she was talking about. When he came closer, he saw that she was a beautiful blonde girl with large green eyes. Susan asked everybody, "What is philosophy?" Most of the people agreed that it is a science about nothing. She countered with "You do not know how exciting it is to read different philosophical books. Philosophy is the science of life and the more you read the more you understand who you are, why you are here and what is really important in this life. It teaches us to live in the moment, and do our best for a better future. All our dreams and wishes will materialize in our future. It gives us happiness, luck and love."

Mike was fascinated by what she said. He asked her what she was doing, that she would have what she desired in the future. She told him that she was doing meditations, visualizing and using her imagination. She said that she used to have a dream about being a professor at a university and to teach students about philosophy and life. She wanted to open their minds to the secrets of life, how everything is connected by the miraculous laws of energy. And now, she told Mike, her dream had come true. Susan was now a professor of philosophy at a university. She taught her students to understand life, to be in balance and harmony with the whole world and to believe that anything is possible in this life. We should just listen and trust our inner self. This will bring you joy, happiness and love.

One person asked "What about money? How will all of this dreaming and visualizing, bring someone money?"

Susan responded, "It's a mystery, but money attracts money. The more you have, the more will come to you. This is why rich people seem to get richer and richer and poor people seem to get poorer and poorer. Nobody knows how and why it works this way, but that's simply the way it is. It's a law of energy. Money attracts money, happiness attracts happiness and luck attracts luck. So, if in the present moment, you have no money, happiness or luck, you must imagine that you already have these things, and all of this will be given to you. Don't ask why, just believe."

Mike told Susan that she was a wonderful person, and that he enjoyed being around her. But, her knowledge and experience of life made him feel inferior. He asked her if he could have her phone number, that he might have a cup of coffee with her someday so that he could talk to her more. Susan said, "Sure, why not?"

The next night, Mike sat by his piano trying to compose music but something was just not right. He could not compose because nothing was coming into his mind. He tried to meditate and visualize, but his mind was racing with one thought after another about his life. Since he could not compose, he went to another room to watch TV, but nothing caught his interest. He felt bored. He began to feel depressed. Then, Mike thinks about Susan (the philosophy girl}, and gives her a call. She was glad to hear from him, and they arranged to meet. He was not bored anymore. He expected something to happen that night. They met at a small café outside, and had a cup of coffee with some brandy. It was a beautiful summer evening, with a light breeze. They were very relaxed and enjoyed being with each other, just like best friends.

Mike felt like he was connected to her, like she was his best friend. Mike asked her "Do you believe in God?" He didn't know why he asked this, but it was something that he had thought about all his life. And he thought that Susan, who had such a great deal of knowledge about philosophy, might give him some insight.

"Yes" she told him. "But, when I was younger, my

system of belief was much different than it is now. I would go to church every Sunday not thinking about who or what I believed in. I just believed like my parents and grandparents believed, and I thought nothing of it. When I was growing, however, I began to think of it more and more, and wanted to understand just who, or what it is, that I should have faith and belief in. Perhaps that is why I went on to study philosophy at the university."

"So," asked Mike, "Can you tell me why you have belief and faith in God now?"

"Yes" Susan told him, "I am happy that I found the answer. One day, in one of my meditations outdoors, I was visualizing about my future. It was at that moment, my head began to feel warmer and warmer. I looked up and saw a face in the clouds. It smiled at me and looked at me with great affection. I had a feeling of safety and security. I felt that He would take care of me now and always. At that moment, I knew about my present and future.This made me feel extremely happy and comfortable."

"For me, God is a massive amount of energy. It controls our feelings, emotions, thinking and dreams. Therefore, if you give a good amount of good energy, good energy will come back to you in a much greater amount than you gave. The same applies to bad energy. So it is better for everyone to love everything in this world, and themselves. It is the way to be happy, joyful, have fun and make all your dreams come true. Besides, I have an angel on my shoulder and he helps me in everything I do. So, I love God!"

Mike felt love to this girl, and he asked her to his apartment. When they arrived however, something changed. He did not feel the connection between them like he did in the café. Something was just not right, but he didn't know what, and he couldn't understand it. Susan also started feeling uncomfortable, but didn't know why. Trying to break the ice, Mike asked her if she would like a glass of wine. They both had a glass, and then another and more. They wanted to feel comfortable again. They wanted to reestablish the connection they had at the café, but nothing happened. They just got drunk.

They began kissing each other. This led to sex. After this, he realized that their sexual relationship was due to the fact that they had gotten drunk. It was not really love. There was no sexual connection between them. Mike now looked upon her as a friend, not a lover. He knew that they would never have sex again. He told her "You are so beautiful, smart and sexy, but I think it would be better if we were just good friends." Susan had a different feeling. She felt love to him, but she told him that she was happy to have him as a friend. Then, they started to feel comfortable with each other, knowing they were just good friends.

After Susan left, Mike went to his piano room. There, he began to see paintings with the same girl he saw before.

With a tremendous amount of energy he began to compose and couldn't stop until 3:00am. After this, he felt very happy and tired. He slept the whole day and didn't wake up until the next evening. Upon waking, he had the feeling that he was in harmony with himself and the whole world.

CHAPTER 4

Nicole asked herself... *Why can't everything in my real life be just as good as it is in my visualization? I can't have a gallery now, because I have neither the money, nor enough pictures. What do I need to do now to take the first step, so that my dream will come true?* Suddenly, Nicole felt so tired of thinking about all this. All she wanted to do was forget about it and do something different. She decided to call her best friend, Annette. She told her that since they hadn't seen each other for such a longtime, that she would really like to meet and talk with her. Annette told Nicole that she had plenty of time to spend with her, because her boyfriend was currently working.

They met in a mall and just went from store to store, not intending to buy anything in particular. Since they had not seen each other for such a long time, they had a lot to tell each other about what was happening in their lives. Nicole asked Annette, "Are you happy with your boyfriend?"

"Not really" answered Annette, "but I just don't like being alone and without anybody."

Nicole said, "I couldn't live with a man whom I didn't

love with all my heart and soul. All the time I have the feeling that there is somebody very special in this world, and that someday I will meet him."

On that, Annette said, "You can't spend your entire life waiting for someone special to come along. If you never meet any man, you will always be alone."

"Sometimes I have a certain vision," said Nicole. "In it, I see a handsome young man, with brown hair and blue eyes. I hear beautiful music in this vision. Afterwards, everything seems so colorful and bright. I get so much energy from this, that all I want to do is paint and paint. It makes me feel very special, and I thank God for this."

"My God!" said Annette, "Forget about your dreams and visions, and return to the real world. Go out and meet new people and make new friends. Have fun and enjoy life. You are intelligent and beautiful, both inside and outside. You are so sexy that you will surely meet a good man and be happy with him; and there are a lot of men around. My boyfriend has a friend who is very nice and single. He's an engineer and makes good money. Sometimes we all go out together and have a very good time. Why don't you come out this weekend with us?"

"Okay" said Nicole. "Just don't tell him about me." Then, they went shopping. They just bought small things. Nicole bought her favorite perfume, Dolce & Gabbana Light Blue and Annette bought mascara.

Nicole was so happy and excited about this meeting, that she came home and felt joyful. Then, she called her mother and told her about this meeting, but she didn't tell her about her dreams and visions. She never told her mother the secrets and special thoughts that she had, because she would never understand them. Her mother said, "You should never sit home alone all the time. You should be thinking about your future." She said, "You should marry, have a couple of children and build a family. Women come into this world to bear children. Leave all the arts to men." Nicole didn't like hearing this. She only called her mother to tell her she was going out with her friends. She thought that this would make her mother happy. Nicole was dreaming and had a vision about a man who loved the arts, and with whom she would be in complete harmony with. With him she saw a creative future and happiness.

Nicole put on her best dress and some Light Blue perfume. She got in her Chevrolet Malibu, which was dark blue, and drove to one of her favorite restaurants called SAMURAI. She really liked Japanese food. The cooking was quite spectacular, and the food was of very high quality. Annette was waiting for her with the friend of her boyfriend. She smiled and was happy to see her. The man's name was Steve. "Hello" said Steve to Nicole, "It so nice to meet you." He was handsome, tall, in good shape, blond and had a very good smile. Nicole liked him from the first moment. It was a wonderful dinner, a great time and good food. Steve asked Nicole for her phone number, which she gave him and she said,

"I look forward to hearing from you soon."

CHAPTER 5

Nicole went back to her apartment. She was very relaxed and began watching an old romantic movie, when her mother called. She asked Nicole about the meeting. Nicole told her briefly about what happened this weekend, and after that she told her mother, "I love you" as she usually did and returned to the movie. The next day Steve called and asked if they could go out together. Nicole told him that Saturday would be very good. She found it very easy to talk to him.

The next morning Monday, Nicole went to her studio which was a small room in her apartment. With a brush in hand, she began to have thoughts about her meeting with Steve, like what she would wear and what they might talk about. These thoughts made her a bit nervous and worried. She called her mother and told her about her date with Steve. Her mother was very excited, and gave her a lot of recommendations. Nicole went back to her canvas, but she couldn't paint. She just sat there staring at the canvas. Something was wrong. She had no dreams or visualizations in her mind. She felt so empty that she decided to watch TV.

She began to surf the channels on TV and came upon

one that was very interesting to her. The program dealt with how to reprogram your brain. The man on TV said that if you feel unhappy, unlucky and that everything is going wrong, you need to reprogram your brain. One must think positive and find something positive in everything. You should find out exactly what you want in your future and concentrate on those thoughts. Repeat these thoughts every morning when you wake up and every night before you go to bed.

Everyone has a lot of thoughts. They come one after another, never stopping. If you try to stop and look at each thought, your mind will relax. During this time, think about your thoughts of your future dreams. This does not happen immediately. You must be very passionate about this and keep repeating it. The man said "If you really want to have something in your life, you must believe that you already have it, and it will be given to you." He said, "It's a mystery. Nobody understands how it works, but it does." Nicole was very excited about this program. She laid in bed for a long time, thinking about this program, and fell asleep.

On Tuesday morning, she woke up and began to follow this program, thinking about her dreams of her future, and repeating this. After a cup of coffee, she went to her studio. Again, she just stared at the canvas and nothing happened. This happened every day until Saturday. It was just the anticipation of something to come.

On Saturday morning she woke up with good

thoughts. She felt that something must happen today, something very important and special. She felt that big changes were about to take place in her life. In her closet she found her favorite dress, which was turquoise, white high heeled shoes and sprayed on some Light Blue perfume. She was very excited about her date with Steve.

They went to a park where they walked and talked. Steve did most of the talking, and talked mostly about himself. Apparently he liked sports, because that's all he talked about. He told Nicole that when he was younger, he participated in all kinds of sports, and that was all he watched on TV. Nicole finally asked him what he did for a living, and his plans. He told her that he was an engineer and made good money. He wanted to find the right girl, get married, buy a good home and have 3 children. His wife would be a homemaker, staying at home, taking care of the kids and doing the cooking and cleaning. In the evening, they would watch TV together in a beautiful, very clean and cozy home. On his days off he would work in the yard, help his wife with some things at home and have some quality time with the kids. He would save money for a yearly vacation, and take a trip to somewhere different every year.

Listening to him, Nicole thought that he seemed like he could be the right person. With this kind of man, every woman would feel safe and happy with this routine. *But what about me? Will I be happy if I choose this style of life and routine?* She stopped thinking and went back to listening to Steve. Steve kept talking about how he would teach different kinds of sports to his children. "They will enjoy this and they will watch all kinds of sports on TV. This will help the children in practicing their favorite sports."

All the time during their date Steve did all the talking and Nicole began to feel tired. She felt as if they were moving further and further apart from each other. She told him, "It was very nice to spend time with each other and talking to you, but now it is late, and I have to go home."

Steve asked Nicole, "Could I call you and we can meet again? I was very happy to talk to you, and I get the feeling that you are very special to me."

"Sure," answered Nicole, "Just feel free to call me."

When Nicole returned home she called her mother. Her mother asked how her date went with Steve. Nicole told her that she had a good time and he seemed to like her. He is thinking about his future. "Good," said her mother. "That's exactly what you need. I am so happy for you now, and hope you will continue dating him."

Nicole said, "Okay, will do."

Feeling very bored, Nicole turned on the TV. However, something was different. Everything started to change. She began to hear music, and saw the same face of the man with blue eyes. She felt a connection with this face and this music. A lot of energy came to her. This made her feel very happy. She had a desire to go to her small studio, but she did not know what she would do there. Nevertheless, it was the only place she wanted to be at this time, and she was absolutely sure she would never see Steve again.

CHAPTER 6

Mike sat by his piano, but couldn't compose because he had no musical feeling, and no vision came to him. He began to feel the doldrums, but Susan (the philosophy girl), came to his mind and he gave her a call. She was glad to hear from him, and they arranged to meet. They really enjoyed seeing each other. They went to a small café outside, and had a cup of coffee with some brandy. It was a beautiful summer evening, with a light breeze. They were very relaxed and enjoyed being with each other, just like best friends.

Susan said "All the time I ask myself, why is there so much negativity in life like jealousy, thievery and murder? Why do so many people get satisfaction from bad things happening to others? Why are some people rich and happy, while others are very poor and unhappy? Usually I tell my students that the world needs balance. There is good energy and bad energy. It reminds me of the legend of Pandoras's box. When she opened the box, she released all the bad energy in the world. It reminds me of yin and yang, good and evil, black and white, God and the Devil."

Mike replied, "That's a very interesting concept. I

never thought about this, but it makes sense and I will give it some thought." Mike said, "I don't have much time, but I'd like to meet with you again, and talk to you about other things. I feel like I can talk freely with you about anything."

"It was very nice to talk to you, and I'm sure we will see each other soon. I'm looking forward to it. Bye, see you later," said Susan.

Mike was in a very good mood when he came home. He went to the room where the piano was, and suddenly he had a vision of the girl with the pictures. Mike began to compose music as fast as he could breathe. When he finished, he noticed that he got a lot accomplished, and this made him feel very good. Afterward, he had something to eat, watched a little TV and then went to bed.

CHAPTER 7

The next day he felt empty. He always had this feeling after composing. He felt like he had to talk to someone, so he called his friend Max, and asked him if they could hang together tonight. Max told him that he knew a couple of girls (Connie and Britney), and he would ask them if they could all go out together. They all met outside a coffee shop. Connie had dark blue eyes, dark brown hair and Britney had brown eyes, dishwater blonde hair. It was a beautiful July evening, and they spent a great deal of time outside the small café enjoying the good weather and engaging in people watching. Connie looked into Mike's eyes and smiled at him. Mike smiled at her too, and said, "You have very pretty eyes, and you seem like a very nice person. I'd like to talk to you more, so that I get a better understanding of you."

She said, "You're a very good looking guy also, and I'd enjoy talking to you."

Mike asked her, "Would you like to come to my apartment, and have something to eat and drink?"

She said, "That sounds good to me!" They told the others that they were leaving and said their goodbyes.

On the way to his apartment they bought a bottle of wine, and held and kissed each other. When they arrived at his apartment, Mike ordered a pizza and opened the bottle of wine, and poured each a glass. They drank some wine, and Mike played and sang while they waited for the pizza. Mike stopped playing when the doorbell rang. He opened the door, and it was the delivery boy with the pizza. Mike poured more wine, and they enjoyed the pizza with it. After the pizza, Mike went back to the piano and played some more. Connie came up behind him, and held him. Mike turned to her and kissed her. They were both a little drunk from the wine and they kissed each other more and more which led to sex. After spending the night with her, Mike felt he would like to be alone. After looking at the girl, who didn't look as good to him as she did the night before, he said to her "I'm sorry, but I have to leave for a meeting right now, and I'll call you later."

Connie cleaned herself up, kissed him and said, "I really enjoyed spending time with you, and I'll wait for your call." Mike called her a taxi, and she left. Mike never called her again.

For a while he just slept, watched some TV and basically did nothing. Soon the Central Park Summerstage Pop music festival was coming to his area and he needed to have new songs and music done for the band on time. But, he had no energy. He just wanted to be lazy and do nothing. Max called him and told him that he was having another party at his home, and that he invited some new girls that he met in the University library. Mike really liked visiting Max's house. It was a large, two level home with 5 bedrooms and a pool in the back. When he got closer to Max's home he could hear music and laughter. In a good mood and very excited, he stepped quickly into the house.

When he arrived, the party was well under way. Some people were drunk, and others were smoking. All the bedrooms were being used, and other couples were waiting to use them. Mike's attention was caught by a blonde girl with bright, hazel eyes. To him, she was very sexy. She approached him and asked if he would like a glass of wine, and he said he would like that. After several glasses, they went to a bedroom. The bedroom was a mess but they didn't care and paid no attention to it. After some incredibly good sex, they returned to the living room where there were a lot people drinking, eating and laughing. They had a great time.

With a big headache, Mike crawled home. He slept all day, and until 3a.m. the next morning. Upon waking, he had the same vision of the girl and the pictures. He thought she must be an angel. This vision gave him a great amount of energy. He went to his studio and composed music until that evening. Everything he composed was because of this vision. The vision was always the same and every time it repeated itself, he composed.

CHAPTER 8

After painting some pictures, Nicole sat and relaxed in her small studio. She thought to herself, *It's such a mystery. Why can I only paint when I have the vision of the man with blue eyes and the sound of beautiful music?* Nicole couldn't find an answer to this question, so she went to the kitchen, made a turkey sandwich with iced tea for lunch and went to the living room. She opened a TV table, turned on the TV and relaxed to a music channel with lunch.

Sometimes with friends Nicole would go to concerts and music festivals. She enjoyed listening to music. It always left her with good ideas, a good mood and a good feeling about everything. Such events made her feel very happy. Nicole remembered that Annette told her that they would attend the upcoming pop music festival in Central Park with several others. Nicole called Annette and asked her exactly when the festival would be. They had a small conversation and Annette told her the festival would be this Friday, and Annette said, "My friends and I will wait for you at the park entrance at 5:00pm."

When Nicole arrived at Central Park, she saw Annette

waiting for her with two men Tony and Nick. They were surprised to see such a beautiful girl and they introduced themselves to her. They told her that they were glad she was able to join them, and together, they went to Summerstage, which was at the heart of Central Park. The festival had already started, but they were lucky to find places to sit. At this time, a man of medium height, black hair and blue eyes was singing. When he was singing, it was like he was not real. He was flying with the music, and she felt like she was flying with him, and at this moment she had a special feeling and emotion to him. When the festival was over, she returned to reality.

After the festival, they all enjoyed a good dinner at a steakhouse. The steak was cooked to perfection, and they all had salad and red wine. They had similar tastes and it was a wonderful dinner. Tony told some funny stories and everybody laughed. He wanted to display his comical side to Nicole, because he really liked her. Everybody had a good time. As they were leaving, Tony asked Nicole if he could have her phone number, so he could call her sometime and Nicole obliged.

Afterwards, Nicole returned home in a good mood and she turned on the TV. Later, she called her mother and told her about Tony. Her mother was always happy when she met a new man. She dreamed that her daughter would get married, just like every mother does. Mothers always wish for their children to have a great future, but kids usually see things differently than their mothers. They have their own dreams, desires and wishes, and to build their own destiny. Nicole ended the conversation with her mother in the manner she usually did by saying, "I love you." She began to watch a romantic movie, and fell asleep. Nicole dreamt she was in love with somebody but, she couldn't see his face or body. She only sensed him. The dream seemed so real. Nicole woke up in the morning with the same repeating vision of the young man and the beautiful sound of music. She went to her studio and began to paint.

CHAPTER 9

Mike's life seemed so routine. Everyday seemed the same and he was constantly worried about composing new songs for the next Summerstage pop festival. The band depended on him to have new songs done on time. He could never relax. To do so, would leave him feeling guilty that the music was not completed. He couldn't let the band down, because he loved the band. They were a very good group of people, like his best friends. Mike said to himself, *Soon we will all meet, and I will show them some of my new songs. But, why can I only compose and create new songs when I have the same repeating vision?*

The band manager called Mike and told him about a band meeting the next day at 6p.m. All day Mike tried to compose, but he had no vision, so no new music. Then, he said to himself that he had already written enough songs so far. *I will have something to eat and go to bed early. I must be fresh and energetic for this very important meeting.* However, he went to bed late, and slept until the afternoon. Mike woke up in a good mood and had a lot of energy for the meeting.

All the members of the band were really happy to get

together and they gave each other high fives. They began to play, and Mike sang his song. The manager thought that it was great. He told Mike, "You are so talented and the band is fantastic. I am so glad to be your manager. We will make a lot of money. Wow!!!" Everybody congratulated each other, especially Mike, for a job well done. They went to an outdoor café, in a place where the young people hung out in the middle of the summer. After a very hot day they drank beer and cocktails. They enjoyed the cool evening and were happy to see each other.

The manager told Mike "You are doing great, but it will not be enough for the festival. You are responsible for many more songs.

He replied, "Oh yes. I realize this, and I will do my best." At the same time, some girls who were nicely dressed came to the café. Smiling and laughing, they sat down close to the band. They were so young, fresh and ready for love, that the boys forgot all about music and the festival. They asked the girls if they could buy them some drinks, and the girls agreed to this. The boys in the band quickly moved their chairs and joined their tables. They all had a lot of laughs, told jokes and had a good time together.

Two of the girls who were best friends, went with Mike to his apartment. There, they drank a lot, and Mike sang old songs for them. They became so drunk and excited, that they began to kiss Mike and each other. It was a menage et trois.

The next morning Mike didn't remember what happened, but he had a very big headache and his whole body ached. Mike just figured that he would take a couple of aspirins and that he would be ready for work. But, he was worried about his ability to compose. Mike really needed something bright and clean at that moment. That is what the vision of the girl, who he believes to be an angel with beautiful pictures, provided him. Mike thought to himself *Even though I've had a lot of good looking girls, why can't I remember them or want to be with them more than one night? I can only remember and think about the girl from my vision. All my feelings are for her. Sometimes I think about other girls, but it's different. It's like thinking about a best friend or sister...there is no chemistry there.*

The rest of the day nothing happened. He had no vision. Mike sat in front of his piano for awhile and played a little something, and then he went to the computer to check his email. There were many jokes written to him by his friends. This put him in a better mood. Every morning, he read the news and other interesting stories. He also loved animals. It was his dream to have a tiger at home, but he knew that this would never happen. He had to settle for a tabby cat. Some of his friends liked hunting and fishing, but he would have nothing to do with such activity. He loved animals too much. Mike even gave regular contributions to the Humane Society.

At about 3a.m that morning, he received the repeating

vision. He quickly went to the piano and composed with great enthusiasm until noon. After that, he felt very happy, as if he had accomplished something very important. He also felt very tired and went to bed. When he was lying in bed, he thought about the girl in his vision. She was so close to him that he could smell her perfume, her hair, her fresh body and he could feel a sexual connection between them. He was lusting for her, and it blew him away. With these thoughts, he fell asleep and had good dreams.

CHAPTER 10

Mike enjoyed playing in front of a crowd at a concert because of all the energy, both from the band, and the crowd. However, at this festival it was different somehow. It was a mystery. He had the unusual feeling that girl from his vision, that he had such an intimate connection to, was in the crowd. Wanting to understand this unusual feeling he thought of Susan, the philosophy professor. Perhaps she could help him understand it more clearly. When he got home, he called her. She picked up the phone really fast, as if she was expecting his call. He asked her if they could meet, and as usual, she was free at that time.

They kissed when they met. Mike felt very relaxed and comfortable around her. It was a warm evening, and a good time to sit outside and relax at a small cafe. When they sat down, Mike told Susan about the feeling he had at the concert, and he said to her, "Since you are a professor of philosophy, you have more knowledge about life and it's feelings and I thought you might be able to give me some advice, or your opinion about this."

She told him, "I understand your desire to find the

answer to this feeling. I've struggled to find an answer to various feelings I've had during my life. Whenever these feelings came to me, I used all my knowledge and experience to try to find explanations concerning them...what they were and what caused them. After all my thinking, and trying to rationalize my feelings, I finally found the answer. It's a mystery, and because it's a mystery, there is no explanation. It's just what it is."

In return, Mike said, "Thank you very much, Susan. That helped me a lot. Now I know that I should just live with these feelings, and not be concerned about what caused them." After that, they felt very happy and carefree. They generally told jokes and made fun talk, like children with no worries or cares.

Then, Mike said "Tell me, you teach your students philosophy and you get some ideas from this. Why do you like to do this? Why is this exciting to you?"

She replied, "You know, when I tell a story to my students, it's like I've broadened their horizons. I've opened a door that allows them to see more in life. It's like I've added a new dimension. Suddenly, things that were routine and nothing to them are now very important. It changes their outlook about life. Their brains become filled with meaningful thoughts instead of junk. So, you can see now how important it is that one has a clear mind, that she or he might see more clearly, which can help one make a proper decision. What matters is the truth, not whether one is right or wrong."

"Thoughts about the mysteries of life make me think of Carlos Castaneda," said Mike. "He wrote a fantastic series of classic books about Indian sorcery. They can make you realize that there may be an alternate reality, that one may see things from difference sides, thus making a person find the right and proper way to achieve his or her desires and goals. They have to do with dreams, adventure, mystery and an entirely different way of thinking. I am reminded of a certain passage in one of his books about dreaming and being able to control one's dreams. There are many thoughts and ideas from his writings that give me inspiration for my compositions."

Susan said, "I am really surprised to hear you talk about Castaneda. I am familiar with his books. They truly exited me. I'm very happy that you have read these books and now I feel a stronger connection to you. In one of my philosophy classes I talked of Castaneda's life style and way of thinking. This captured the interest of many of my students. To see their reaction made me grateful for my job. I couldn't imagine doing anything else. I try to steer everybody's brain to focus on happiness, love, balance and harmony. It's a fantastic way of life. I'm glad that in my life there is no negativity such as jealousy, lying and backstabbing."

Mike said, "I enjoyed our conversation today, and I look forward to many more. I'm a lucky man to have such a good friend. I'm sure I'll talk to you soon." Susan thought to herself, *I love him more and more, but I must regard him as a wonderful friend.* They kissed each other, and with good feelings toward each other, they went their separate ways.

CHAPTER 11

Nicole was painting in her studio. She tried one color after another, but she was not happy. She mixed a few colors together and got a very nice color, which she liked very much. This put her in a very good mood, like she had attained something that she really wanted. She finished the picture and thought to herself *That's one more picture to go into my future gallery*. It was hard work, and now it was time to relax.

It had become a tradition for Nicole and Annette to meet at Central Park every Friday, to listen to music and enjoy the food. Nicole called Annette to confirm where they would meet. Nicole met with Annette and some of her friends at Wendy's, before they went into Central Park. They went into the park to listen to the bands. They enjoyed listening to the songs from different bands. There were thousands of people, and it was a very exciting and good atmosphere.

Nicole's attention was caught by one boy with dark brown hair and dark blue eyes. She remembered she had seen him at the Summerstage pop festival last Friday. He sang so well, and Nicole felt that he was singing especially for her. Nicole felt a connection to him, like they had known each other for a long time, and that he was very special to her. Nicole thought to herself, *who is this boy and why do I feel like I know him.* After listening to different bands, they strolled around the park, and discussed their opinions of the different bands, their music and the singers. It was a great evening. They enjoyed each other's company, and when they became very tired, they all went home.

In the early morning, Nicole received the recurring vision again. She realized that the boy in her vision also looked like the singer that she saw at Central Park, to whom she felt such a strong connection to. He had the same eyes, the same face and played the same music that so inspired her to paint. She couldn't believe that it was all in her mind. While she lay in bed, she thought about her vision and other things came to her mind. One of these thoughts was to clean and rearrange her studio. Nicole got up, and after breakfast, she went to her studio to rearrange it. However, because she had the vision in the morning, she began to follow her emotions and feelings, and started to paint instead.

After painting, she returned to the real world, and began to rearrange her studio. In doing so she picked up a large, heavy picture and got a severe pain in her lower back. She went to a doctor who told her that she had a strong body, and with the proper therapy, she would soon be okay. The doctor was originally from the Philippines. His name was Joe. He had a very good personality and was quite handsome. He made Nicole feel very comfortable and relaxed. She trusted him. Nicole asked him what made him decide to be a doctor, and he told her that ever since he was a young boy, he could always feel the pain of other people and he always wanted to help. Then, Joe said, "So, I went to the USA to study to be a doctor. That is all I ever wanted to be and I thank God for this opportunity and His support. I truly believe in Him."

"You know," said Nicole, "I feel absolutely the same way. I've always painted, and I believe that is what God intended for me to do. I can feel His support also. When I'm painting I feel His energy being channeled through me. During these creative moments I hear beautiful music. It's like being in a trance and it excites me very much."

Joe told Nicole, "I really want to see your pictures. I feel that you have a lot of talent and will have a very bright future."

"Thank you very much," said Nicole. "When I have my own gallery, I will invite you to visit, and I will be very happy to see you again."

For a couple of weeks she had therapy, and talked with the doctor about life and relationships. He recommended some exercises for her to do at home. Soon, Nicole's health was back to normal, and she returned to painting pictures and having visions. Often she dreamt about her own gallery, which entertained many people. She also dreamt about the boy with blue eyes, who was in her visions that were accompanied by the sound of beautiful music.

CHAPTER 12

Mike woke up in a bad mood. He slept for a long time, but he felt like he could have slept more. He wondered why he felt like this sometimes, but he also realized that he usually felt like this after composing music for an extended period of time. Mike also knew that it was not good to wake up in a bad mood, because nothing good would happen to him. He thought that he must change his mood before he became melancholy, and the best thing for him would be to call Susan again. He called Susan and they arranged to meet in the same small café.

Mike asked Susan, "Do you believe in the laws of the universe?"

Susan said, "Yes, I do. I believe that if one emanates bad energy, more negative energy will come back to him or her. The same is true for positive energy. If one gives off positive energy, he or she will be blessed with happiness, luck and money. However, the goal of creative people is not the attainment of money, but rather, to be given the unfathomable wonder of the universe. They become channels of creativity and talent. Because of this, they will be given money, (a lot of money!) The Universe will take care of that. Real creativity can be like fine wine, both exquisite and very expensive.

Mike replied, "The same can be said of rock music of the '60s, '70s and '80s. It can still touch people of any age. For instance, many of the Beatle's tunes of the '60s were very good and can still be heard today. Another group that made its debut during that time was the Rolling Stones. They're still making music today, and have only gotten better over time, and Elvis is like champagne. There were also other very fine artists, such as Jimi Hendrix and Janis Joplin, but they died before they matured. The '70s and '80s saw the upstart of many good bands and much talent, but only one group bedazzled everybody, Cream. Their talent was incredible. Eric (slow hand) Clapton was a fantastic guitarist and Ginger Baker was a great drummer. And, through all those decades, there was Motown."

Susan said, "Everything that you spoke of is very interesting. I also get great enjoyment from the music of that time period."

Mike asked Susan, "What is the true meaning of the arts to you?"

Susan responded, "To me, the arts are emotions and feelings given to the people. It connects very intimately with them and allows them to better understand themselves. It helps them see what they truly desire and gives them a reason for their existence."

Then Mike asked, "What is your opinion about money?"

Susan answered, "Money is like a magnet. It can both attract and repel. Money attracts money, and yet once one has it, it can be difficult to keep. Yet, all one has to do is believe that he or she already has it and it will be given. It's a mystery. However, most people are unable to believe that they have a lot of money when they don't. This can also be said about happiness, luck and success. It is so hard to believe, and yet, so easy."

Mike said, "Yes, I can understand how it would be very difficult to believe that you have something when you don't. This is probably also true when it comes to your state of mind. If you are in a bad mood, you cannot immediately return to a normal state of mind, but it must be done. I am very happy, and in very good mood when I am creating music. I feel like I was born for this."

Susan told him that she liked his way of thinking, and that it was very similar to the way she thought. She told him that she was interested in his feelings and thoughts when he created music. Susan told Mike, "I always have an interest to the reasoning process of artists and musicians. Whenever I meet with one, I always ask them about their thoughts and feelings during their creative moments." She told him that they responded, "We don't have any thoughts, we just feel we have to do this."

CHAPTER 13

Mike was unable to compose music, so he just wandered around his apartment, feeling empty and no thoughts in his mind. It was usually when he felt like this, that his friend Max would call. That in itself is a mystery. There seems to be some sort of connection between people who are close to each other. One knows when the other is in depression, a bad mood or in poor health. Perhaps there is a kind of electrical signal which sends information on a mental level. Consequently, Max called at this moment, reaffirming Mike's belief.

Max asked him, "What's going on? What's the good word?"

Mike said, "Same old, same old."

Max said, "I'm having a party tonight and you're more than welcome." This was like a wake- up call for Mike.

He said, "That sounds good. I'll be there." Suddenly, Mike seemed like a different person. He began to smile and move faster. He took a shower and spent more time on his hair than usual. Like a new man he left for the party.

When he arrived at the party, there were many people

drinking and smoking. It was chaos. Everybody did what he or she pleased. Mike's attention was caught by a girl sitting by the piano, both playing and singing. He liked this, and listened for a while. He came closer and clapped his hands. He told her, "That's not bad at all! I really enjoy your musical ability. I'd like to hear more." It was country music. It wasn't the type of music that he cared for, but he did enjoy it occasionally when he was driving. She was very good. This girl had talent.

Mike also noticed that she was the type of girl he was usually attracted to. She was a pretty redhead, with hazel eyes, full lips and a very shapely body. The girl's name was Lisa, and she was also gazing at Mike. She thought he was very sexy and handsome. She liked his deep blue eyes. She felt that there was something very special about blue eyes. Mike felt very comfortable just being around her, and listening to her songs. He asked her if she would like to dance, and she said she would love to. As they danced, they did not speak, but just felt and touched each other. There was a connection and chemistry between them. He asked her to come home with him after the party. He told her that in the morning, he would compose a new song which only she would hear. He said, "This will be my gift to you." Mike was a romantic type. He enjoyed giving gifts, like flowers, chocolate and perfume, to girls he liked. The rest of the evening was wonderful.

Mike woke up quite early, and he was taken aback at how beautiful Lisa looked as she slept. Immediately, he went to his piano and composed a new song especially about her. The sound of the music caused her to awaken, and Lisa went to Mike in his studio. There, he sang his song to her. This exited her very much and she kissed him passionately. It was a very special moment between them, and then, Mike made coffee and breakfast. Afterwards, they had to return to their own worlds. Unfortunately, and reluctantly, they kissed and parted. Normally, Mike would pick up a girl at a party, have sex with her, and the next day he would just go back to composing music, and never think of her again. But Lisa was different. He thought about her a lot, and he was sure that he would see her again.

CHAPTER 14

Mike called Susan, one of his best friends, and asked for a meeting. He felt like he could talk to her about anything. They met in a small café, and they sat outside, where they could people watch and converse. Susan started talking about a program she had seen yesterday on the History channel. It was about the military conducting tests on tanks and ships during World War II, to make them become invisible. What made it more incredible was that former soldiers described it. "It was unbelievable," Susan said. "It was like fantasy becoming reality, science fiction becoming fact." They began to imagine that perhaps invisible people were amongst them right now, watching and controlling the world, unbeknownst to others.

Mike said, "Who knows what secrets will become known over time. We don't know what surprises and knowledge will be given to us in the future."

Susan said, "Yeah, it's like a brave new world. My favorite TV channels are History, Science and Discovery, because I always get new information and learn something new from them." She asked, "What are your favorite TV programs, Mike?"

Mike replied, "With another music festival coming up I must be ready. I am so busy composing music, that I have no time to watch TV. However, when I can, my favorite channels are SciFi, NatGeo, and also the Science and History channels."

Susan said, "We have a lot in common. We like the same channels on TV. I like the SciFi channel too." She asked, "Tell me Mike, what do you like about SciFi?"

He answered, "I like it because it deals with things that could happen in the future, like Star Trek and other space stories. It makes me feel as if I'm part of that story, and living in that time. When the story is over, I realize that this could happen someday."

Susan replied "I think the same way, but what about the other channels that capture your interest?"

Mike said "The Science channel deals with the facts from which fiction is conjured in the mind. It seems like new things are being discovered every day, and things that were discovered are now history, which is why I enjoy the History channel. Knowledge of the past gives greater understanding of the present, and what can be in the future. NatGeo allows me to witness the awe and mystery of the world around me. Nature and different cultures are truly amazing. It takes my breath away. This channel makes me want to see the world."

Susan replied, "I like your thoughts about these

channels. I have the same feeling about the programs shown on them." After they finished their coffee and conversation, Mike kissed Susan, and they left.

After meeting with Susan, Mike couldn't wait to get home and compose. He was full of happiness, good feelings and deep emotions, which was usually how he felt before creating a new song. For him, composing was like being at a fork in the road. If you turned one way, the road would lead nowhere. If you turned the other way, it would lead to creativity and wonderful moments. Composing music is border line between reality and mystery, the same as being on the edge of a knife. It was these feelings that he had, which led to creativity and new songs.

When he got home, he quickly went to his piano. Then it happened. He received the vision of the beautiful girl, surrounded by pictures, which always occurred when he began to compose a new song and music. Afterwards, Mike was exhausted and covered with sweat, but feeling very happy that something very important was accomplished. With these thoughts and feelings, he fell asleep.

CHAPTER 15

In her studio, Nicole was surrounded by many pictures. She thought to herself that even though I have a lot of paintings, it is still not enough for a gallery. I need to put in a lot of very hard work, in order to open my own gallery. She realizes it will be difficult, but it is the one thing she wants in her life.

She had a feeling that she needed to be with someone, so she called her friend Annette, and Nicole asked her if they could meet, and go shopping together. Annette said, "Let's do it! I need some new clothes and there could be other things that I might need." Annette was a shopaholic. She loved to shop, and she knew all of the brand names. She always tried to find bargain basement prices on very expensive items, be they clothes, shoes, purses, jewelry or items for her home. Usually she shopped at the mall, but sometimes she could find very good deals at the local T.J. Maxx. Annette had a beautiful big home and she was always moving things and buying decorations to match.

Nicole asked Annette, "Why do you spend all your money on these things?"

Annette responded, "It's my life, and this is what I like to do. On TV, I enjoy watching jewelry shows, designer shows and shows that deal with models on the runway. And, of course, I love men. I love a man with impeccable taste, who knows how to treat a woman right, like a real gentleman. He likes to make a woman happy by taking her to dinner, or getting her something to drink at the right time. He also should be very supportive and helpful." They decided to meet each other at the mall.

Nicole said, "Sounds good. I'll see you there."

Nicole was different. She was in harmony with creativity, painting and her vision. She had the feeling that the boy in her vision, who had blue eyes and was accompanied by wonderful music, was her soul mate. However, sometimes Nicole was like every ordinary girl. She liked to shop, have fun and have boys around. Annette always helped Nicole go to the right places, buy good clothes, quality perfume and everything else that is necessary for young women.

Nicole met Annette at the mall in the afternoon. There were three guys with Annette, and they were laughing, smiling and telling jokes with each other. Nicole was happy to see them, and was glad that Annette was her friend. Together they did a little shopping, and generally had a good time. They came upon a small outdoor café. The boys had beer, and the girls had juice. They just enjoyed the weather and engaged in people watching.

Annette asked Nicole if she would soon have enough paintings to open a gallery. "Soon, hopefully," said Nicole.

One boy (his name was Paul), told Nicole, "My father owns a hall which he rents for all kinds of exhibitions. Perhaps I can be of help."

"That's really interesting. It would be great if my dream were to finally come true," said Nicole.

"Could I see your paintings, so that I can describe them to my father?" Paul asked Nicole.

"Absolutely," she replied.

At her apartment/studio, Nicole showed Paul her paintings and he was very excited by what he saw. "Unbelievable," he said. "I couldn't imagine that your paintings would be so fantastic. This is great. I think I will bring my father to your studio. I want him to see this. I'm sure that he will be very impressed." This made Nicole very happy. Paul looked into her eyes and said, "You are so beautiful, both inside and outside. You are like the girl that I have dreamed about. I would like to know you better. Would you like to have dinner with me this Friday night?"

Nicole answered, "I'd like that very much. Personally, I prefer Japanese."

"Okay," said Paul, "I know a great sushi bar."

The following Friday they met at the sushi bar, and enjoyed very high quality sushi. They had a very good dinner, and spent most of the time discussing about his father coming to her studio. However, the next day Paul called Nicole, and told her that his father (whose name was Norman) had become very ill and had to be hospitalized. "His gall bladder burst. He is lying in a hospital bed right now with all kinds of intravenous tubes in him, and all kinds of medical technological machines around him. He is in a great deal of pain right now, but when he will return to good health, he will visit your studio and see your paintings."

Nicole responded, "I'm sorry to hear this disturbing news about your father. I hope he will be alright."

"Me too," said Paul.

CHAPTER 16

Mike may have had different feelings, emotions and tastes, but his vision always remained the same. It was very stable and never changed. He wished he would have this vision more often, because he always felt very creative, happy and fulfilled afterwards. However, the vision was like an ideal fantasy...so lovely that he wanted to remain there, but he had to return to reality, which was filled with emptiness and unhappiness. It was during this time that he would go out, see friends, have sex or do something to make him feel happy and fill this emptiness.

Mike was trying to decide who to call - Susan (the philosophy professor) or Lisa (the girl he is currently dating). With Susan he feels very comfortable, and her way of thinking gives him energy and makes him more alert. With Lisa, he is very relaxed and has great sex. This makes him want to do something serious, like compose music and be creative. However, to be truly creative he needs to have the vision of the girl and the paintings. He believes that he needs all three of these girls in his life.

Mike needs Susan, because she makes him more

aware. He needs Lisa, because she gives him happiness, joy and good feelings, but he also needs the girl in his vision to make him able to compose music, write songs and sing. These three girls put balance in his life. He couldn't make up his mind which girl to call, and since this dilemma was causing him grief, he decided to call Max.

When he called Max, Max asked him to come over. He told Mike that he had a lot of friends at his house. Mike liked to visit Max's house because he was always very comfortable and relaxed there. When Mike arrived, he was surprised that the only people at Max's house were men. It was a bachelor party! All the guys were drinking beer and whisky, and watching porno movies and playing cards. They were also talking about sports, cars and politics. It was a typical man party. Mike mentioned to them about the upcoming Pop festival and invited everyone there. For the most part, the guys looked forward to being there.

After the party, Mike called Susan because she gave his mind energy, and that is just what he needed at this time. He told her that he missed her, and would like to meet her at the café, where they always met. Susan was very glad to hear from him, because she loved Mike very much. Mike did not know this. Susan realized that he considered them to be just friends, but she wished that he was someone special, more than just a friend. Susan was very attractive, and got a lot of compliments from other men and students, but she only wanted to spend time with someone special. Susan felt that Mike was that someone special that she dreamed about.

They met at their favorite café, where they both ordered a cup of coffee and gazed at each other. Then, Mike asked Susan, for a reason unknown to him, what she thought about the lottery. She said, "Some people seem to be very lucky and win quite often, and then again, there are those who frequently lose. They win a small amount, but they spend a lot of money. What is interesting though, is that those who win a lot of money much of the time, are those who really do not need it," said Susan. "But the lottery is a mystery. Nobody understands how it works. One thing is for sure though, it's a form of gambling, which can be both enjoyable and dangerous. This is quite evident in casinos. Some people can walk away whether they win or lose, and others cannot quit. They have a one track mind. They can only think of winning. They are addicted."

CHAPTER 17

Nicole woke up from a nightmare. She was breathing hard, shaking and covered with sweat. She dreamt that she was being chased by a man who wanted to rape her. He got so close to her that he was going to grab her. At that moment, she woke up screaming. Even though she was a nervous wreck, she was happy that it was just a dream, and that she was home and in bed. This gave her a feeling of comfort. She told herself that everything was okay, got up and made herself a cup of coffee and went to her studio. She was amazed by how many paintings there were. Soon, she would need to find a way to get her own gallery.

Nicole turned on the TV, and happened upon a program about an opera singer who was also an engineer. He opened a construction business which created water fountains that connected music and water. The fountains were beautiful, displaying different speeds and directions, which were able to give one incredible feelings. Nicole began to hear the music which normally accompanied her vision. This became a very creative moment for her. She began to paint as if she were in a trance. She painted pictures of water fountains of different colors, different geometric shapes and varied directions, extremely fast.

Nicole wanted to share her ideas and paintings with someone, so she called Paul and asked him to come over. Paul was ecstatic that she remembered him and asked him over. He really liked this girl, but he saw that all her attention was given to her paintings, and she thought about nothing else. He quickly came to her apartment. When he arrived, she held him and excitedly told him about her paintings of water, and she needed his opinion of the paintings. When Paul came to her studio, he was shocked to see the number of pictures she had painted. He told her, "They are so beautiful. I can feel the energy of the water. The different colors, shapes and directions seem like music. It's fantastic!"

Then Paul said, "Oh, Nicole. You are so beautiful, and such a genius." Nicole was very sensitive, and his words really touched her. Paul held and kissed Nicole. Eventually, Paul said to Nicole, "I believe you have enough paintings now to display in a gallery. My father is doing much better now, so I will talk to him about you, and your paintings. He has his own building which he rents to others for exhibitions. I will ask him if he would be willing to allow you to use it as a gallery. I think it would be a good investment. I would like for the three of us to have dinner together, that we could talk about it."

Nicole answered, "I would love to. It would be like a dream come true to have my own gallery."

The next day, they all met at a fine Italian bistro. Paul's father really liked Nicole. He thought she would be a good fiancée for his son. Norman told Nicole, "I am very interested in learning more about you, your personality and character. I have a feeling that we will work together, but it's good to know about those you are doing business with."

Nicole said, "I'm interested in learning more about you too." Then, their conversation turned to other subjects such as, music, books and the arts.

Paul's father asked Nicole, "What kind of books do you prefer?"

Nicole answered, "I prefer nonfiction novels that deal with history and biographies, but sometimes I like to read mysteries and romance novels." Then Norman asked her what method of painting she liked, and she said that she liked all types of painting, but preferred abstractionism and impressionism. Nicole said, "I once went to the Museum of Modern Art, where I saw a painting by Claude Monet, that when seen from a distance is like a photograph of what he saw at that particular moment. It was called Water Lilies. This really excited me. It made me feel as if I were seeing exactly what he saw at the moment he painted them. After seeing this, I bought a book that showed the paintings of the various artists of the impressionist movement. Besides Monet, I am also quite fond of the works by Renoir and Cezanne. However, I also saw other paintings of abstract art in this museum by Pablo Picasso, Hans Hofmann, Wassily Kandinsky and Kazimir Malevich. Abstractionist artists use of color, texture, lines and geometric forms to display their emotions, feelings, ideas and energy. This type of art captured me. It was like it reached out and grabbed me. It was then that I knew this to be my calling in life."

"Wow," said Norman, "after listening to that, I can see your knowledge and personality. I am sure you are a very talented artist, and I would really like to see your paintings. Next weekend, I will have time, and it would be my pleasure to meet you at your studio. I have the feeling that I will like your paintings, and after we meet I will decide about whether or not to invest the time and money in your gallery."

Paul was extremely happy that his father liked Nicole and was going to see her paintings. He hoped that his father would help her in her quest to realize her dream. Paul knew that his father was a very good businessman, and if he made a decision to start a business, everything would be accounted for, and it would be profitable.

CHAPTER 18

The pop festival was just around the corner and Mike was ready. He had written all the songs, and everyone that had heard them, liked them. But, prior to their performing, the band manager wanted to hear them play, see the program, and it's listing of all the band members. The band was comprised of six people. They were as follows:

Mike - piano and vocals

Chris - bass guitar

Gerry - rhythm guitar

Dave - lead guitar

Jim - drums

Alex - saxophone

They all decided to get together Monday, because that was the best day for everyone, since they weren't sure how long this meeting would take.

Mike reviewed all the songs, and he felt that three of the songs needed some modification. After making the changes, he thought they sounded much better. When the band gets together, they will choose which songs they want to play at the festival. Mike hoped they would choose all the songs, because he really liked them all and they were like a part of him.

On Monday all the band members and the band manager met at an empty garage. They drank beer and began to sing and play music. The band manager said that the music was not only great, but fresh. He told the band that they should practice a lot, and he asked Mike to compose more music, so that they could be considered the best band at the festival. So, Mike returned back to his apartment. After having something to eat, he watched a bit of TV and relaxed a little. Then, Mike went to his studio. As soon as he sat by the piano, the same vision of the girl and the paintings came to him. He began to compose. He worked so hard, that he had no time to do anything else. Work, work, work was all he seemed to do. He knew exactly what needed to be done so that everything was finished in time for the festival. Then, Susan called him.

They hadn't seen each other for a while, and Susan told him that she missed him. Mike was glad to hear from her, and he told her that he missed her too. He said he missed their meetings, their conversations and sharing his thoughts with her. Susan gave him support, and helped him see things more clearly, and have a better understanding of himself. However, he told Susan that he couldn't meet with her at this time, because he had to put the finishing touches on the band's music so that they would be ready for the pop festival, which would be happening very soon. Mike apologized to Susan for this and asked her to come to the festival and bring her friends. He told her that he would try to see her before the festival if he could find the time.

CHAPTER 19

Nicole waited at her apartment for Paul and his father. She cleaned her apartment and studio, and organized all her paintings by themes. She did this so that Paul's father Norman, would have a better understanding of how the gallery should look, and how much space would be needed. Upon looking at her paintings, she realized that she didn't have any paintings of a religious nature. She felt that such paintings should be done before the opening of the gallery. Paul and Norman arrived at her apartment around 5pm., planning to take Nicole to dinner. Paul's father noticed how clean and cozy her apartment was. He liked her even more because of this. After a short conversation, Nicole asked them if they would like anything to drink. Norman asked her if she had any cognac, and Paul chose beer.

When they stepped into the studio, Norman was amazed. He said, "Unbelievable! These paintings are just fantastic! I like them a lot, but there are not enough for my exhibition hall. We will need more. I can see that it will be a huge success. People will love these paintings. They will be attracted to them like a magnet, drawing them closer. They are so bright and full of energy, that people will enjoy them immensely."

Nicole answered, "Thank you very much. I didn't expect that my pictures would mean so much to you. But, I need a little more time because I'd like to put some religious pictures in the center of the gallery, depicting stories from the Bible. This is very important to me, and I hope people who come to the gallery will appreciate this."

Norman embraced Nicole and told her, "We will do whatever you wish." Then he asked her if she would have dinner with him and his son Paul.

Nicole said" Absolutely. I would love to have dinner with the both of you." They decided to have seafood, and went to a Red Lobster restaurant. It was dinner time and the restaurant was very busy, so they had to wait for an empty table. They got a table after twenty minutes. Paul and Norman both ordered crab, and they ordered lobster for Nicole.

CHAPTER 20

Mike got up early. Today the band was supposed to practice and have a meeting with their manager. They met at 5pm, and the manager said, "I hope you are ready for the festival. Let's find out." The band started to play, and Mike sang. The manager was very serious, which made everybody nervous.

When they finally stopped the manager remarked, "Good job. Everyone played well, but the band needs more practice, and Mike needs to compose more and make some changes in the songs. Everything needs to be done in a week."

Mike returned to his apartment, and thought about what the manager said, but he didn't want to think about his responsibilities right now. He felt tired and just wanted to relax. He didn't want to get involved in any serious conversations. He didn't want to think about anything. So, Mike decided to call Lisa, because he felt comfortable and relaxed with her.

Lisa was very glad that he called. She had been waiting quite a while to hear from him. He told her that it was a very special day for him, and that he wanted to see her, and spend some time with her. Mike suggested that they meet at a certain pizzeria. When they met, they held and kissed each other. While they ate, they just smiled at each other and talked very little, and when they did speak, it was about simple things. They felt very comfortable with each other. After eating, they bought a bottle of wine, went to his apartment and enjoyed the rest of the evening together. There, they just melted in each other's arms.

The next day, Mike felt very good and full of energy. He was ready to do something. Mike found something that needed to be done in his apartment. He cleaned the refrigerator, and was happy to get it done. Afterwards, Mike went to the piano and played whatever came to his mind. He felt satisfied and fulfilled, and yet anxious. Since Mike knew the date of the festival, which was soon, and everything was ready, all he could do was wait.

Mike gave Susan a call, because he wanted to be around an intelligent girl, who could carry on a thoughtful conversation. Mike and Susan met in the same café where they usually met. They held each other, and it occurred to him that he loved this girl like a sister. "What's up?" Susan asked him.

"Same old, same old," said Mike. "I went shopping this week and bought some clothes, shoes and cologne. I hate shopping, but sometimes you gotta do what you gotta do. That's life."

"Most of the time, we do what we wanna do, not what we need to do." Susan said, "The best you can do, is try to enjoy what you are doing, give it your best, and imagine that it's exactly what you wanted to do at that moment."

Mike said, "I like what you said. It's so simple, and yet, so profound. Sometimes, someone does something that seems so easy, but only when that person is finished doing it, does he or she realize that it can be very difficult for someone else. Only after practice and experience is it easy."

She replied, "For sure, knowledge and experience are very important in all aspects of life. A person shouldn't be afraid of doing anything new, especially in the business world. If someone is afraid to start something new, his or her dreams and wishes may never come true. When you are young, you have to learn and study a lot, and get as much knowledge as possible. This will help you in anything you undertake in life. You should also have a strong belief system. Knowledge, and believing in what you do, will always bring you luck and success."

Mike said to Susan "I'm so happy that we met and had this conversation. I feel more confident now, and I have a greater understanding of my purpose in this life."

Susan said, "You are a very good person Mike, and I enjoy being with you. Your attention to my thoughts helps me to see more clearly. When I speak with you, I am able to see things from different perspectives."

Grateful for the comment, Mike said, "Thank you very much. I hope I will always be of help to you, and you will always be my best friend."

"Thank you, thank you, thank you. You make me feel so special, and I know that after I share my thoughts with you, that I will feel like a new person, and be able to see things more clearly," said Susan.

They drank their coffee and didn't speak any more. They felt comfortable just being with each other. Usually, people tend to feel uncomfortable to be with each other and not say anything. They feel like they have to talk about something, but not Mike and Susan.

CHAPTER 21

Norman's decision that Nicole did not have enough paintings was actually fortunate for Nicole, because she wanted to include some religious paintings in her collection. She felt that religion was a very important aspect in many people's lives. It was her desire to shed a new light on the truth, so that God and believing could be perceived in new ways, but she needed to have a creative moment. This usually occurred when she had the vision of the boy with blue eyes and the music.

Nicole sighed, and thought about these paintings. No sooner did she begin to think about this, that the vision took place. Again, she saw the same vision, and with a burst of energy, she began to paint one picture after another. Within a short period of time, she had all the paintings that she needed to open the gallery. Nicole thought that her dream was finally about to come true.

She said to herself that she was really happy that she could do what she liked. On the other hand, some of her friends didn't know what they really wanted to do. They just followed the standard path of going to college, choosing a profession, and basically doing something that they really didn't enjoy for the rest of their lives. There were some, however, who chose a profession, and were really happy with it. Granted, there are some people who know exactly what they want to do in life, but they cannot afford it, or they are afraid that they can't do it. Then again, there are those who do nothing of value whatsoever. All they care about is sleeping, eating and partying. They tend to take advantage of everyone around them, especially their parents. It is a vicious circle, and can lead to depression. She thought to herself, *I am very fortunate to be doing something that I like. It's great!*

After painting all the pictures with a religious theme, Nicole cleaned her studio and organized the paintings. Afterwards, she walked from one painting to another, and stopped briefly before each picture. Each painting gave her the feeling and emotions that she had during her creative moments brought on by the vision. She put great value in each painting, as if they were a part of her life. It was similar to looking at photos that were taken during previous parts of life. They remind one of what happened to him or her, and his or her dreams and wishes at different times.

Nicole got lost in the thought that when people see old pictures of themselves, they realize that when they were younger, they didn't believe they could accomplish some things because they seemed so difficult and impossible. When they got older however, they could see that such things were really nothing. All things are possible. All you have to do is believe in yourself. Your wishes and dreams can come true if you follow all the necessary steps.

CHAPTER 22

After talking with Susan on the phone, Mike thought to himself, *this is the first time that I can remember, that I do not want to compose. It seems like hard work for me.* He just wanted to go out with Susan, relax and do some people watching, like they had been doing for quite a while now, and talk with her about something interesting to both of them.

They met at the same café where they always met. It was a special place for them to sit, talk, relax and watch people. Mike kissed Susan and said "I'm so glad we could meet. I look forward to talking to you about different things. I like your intelligence. Getting together with you is different than others who just sit together, kill time, and talk about nothing of any importance. They can't stand to be alone with themselves. They find it boring. They get together, over and over again, to the point that it becomes routine. So, if someone at work or school asks them how they are doing, they say ok, but perhaps they aren't. All they really did was engage in their routine."

Susan responded, "They don't like change in their lives. Change scares them, so they find it difficult to accept anything new. Thus, they don't like to take risks. To truly love someone can also be fearful, because it carries with it many emotions, which can result in a lot of pain and worry. So, they find it better to return to their routine and kill such emotions. It's easier to just not deal with them."

Mike was different. He was a creative person, and liked spontaneity in his life. He did whatever he felt like doing at the moment. There were times when he felt like composing and writing songs, and other times when he felt like relaxing, meeting with friends or watching TV. However, this was a trying time for him. He had to make some changes and corrections to the music he wrote for the festival. And having to have this done at a specific time made him nervous. Mike said to himself, *you have to do this*. So, he just sat by the piano waiting for something to happen, but it never did.

So, he called the band manager and told him that the changes could not be done by the time that he wanted. Mike promised him that all would be done one day before the festival. The manager reluctantly agreed, but he told Mike that if there was anything that either he or the band didn't like, he wouldn't have any time to make the necessary changes. He'd have to take that risk. Getting a few extra days made Mike happy and relieved.

CHAPTER 23

Nicole had a dream in which she saw a large gallery with all her paintings. A lot of people were viewing and discussing her paintings. They were pleased to be there. Nicole woke up and thought to herself, *It all seemed so real. I wish this would happen soon, and my dream becomes reality.* She couldn't wait for something to happen to make all her wishes, desires and dreams to come true, but she also knew, that she needed to be active, and do everything possible to make her wishes and dreams a reality. Our life presents moments which allow us to build our future, and that brings us closer to realizing our dreams and wishes. So, we should enjoy every present moment. They give us harmony, balance and happiness.

Nicole felt like calling either Annette or Paul. It didn't take her long to decide who to call. She realized that she didn't want to go shopping and engage in small talk about unimportant things, so she decided to call Paul. She enjoyed being around him and sharing her thoughts with him. He looked sexy to her, and he treated her right. He gave her the attention she needed. At that very moment, Paul called Nicole and asked her to come to his apartment. Paul did exactly the same thing that she wanted to do.

When she arrived, they kissed and held each other. Paul asked her what she would like to drink. Nicole said "I'll have a cosmopolitan, thinking that he would not have it in his apartment. But he did! Paul chose to have Crown Royale and club soda. After serving the drinks, Paul put on some music. As they sipped their drinks and made small talk, Paul asked Nicole to dance. As they danced, Paul held Nicole tightly and gave her compliments and told her very good words. This made Nicole feel very happy and sensual. They passionately kissed each other and had extremely good sex.

Usually, when a man and woman make love, they tend to see each other in a different way. The relationship between Nicole and Paul moved to a new level. They were now closer than before. Like most girls, Nicole felt that she had finally found love. Nicole was happy now that she had a boyfriend and perhaps they would someday get married. Most often, girls who have a close boyfriend think of this, and this thought also came to Nicole. She was fixated about a boy with blue eyes, like the boy in her vision. Paul also had blue eyes, so Nicole threw all her love and hope his way.

When Nicole returned to her apartment, she began to have doubts. She realized that she really didn't know who Paul was. She didn't know about his life, or what he was really thinking. He never talked about his job, his friends or what he did and didn't like. When Nicole asked him what he did for a living, he told her that he was in business with friends, but he never told her what that business was. He never told her that he loved her. He just talked about how beautiful and nice she was, and how interesting her paintings were. But, like some girls believe, if they have sex with a man, it must be true love. Nicole thought the same way.

CHAPTER 24

Since Mike had a few days before the festival to relax and do what he wanted, he decided to call Susan and ask her to meet with him when she had some free time. As usual, Susan was waiting for him to call. She was always ready to meet with him. She really loved him and could not wait to meet with him. They met at the same small café where they usually had their meeting, and they both ordered coffee. This had become a tradition between them, because Susan liked this place.

Mike told Susan that he had a few days before he had to have everything done to his festival music, but right now, he wanted to take a break for a couple days before he got back to work. Then, Mike told Susan, "Today and this evening, I want to be with you." Susan liked hearing this and was ready to show him a very good time. Susan wanted to be more than just a friend, she wanted to be Mike's lover. She didn't want to show her true feelings about this, so to be just friends was good for her too.

Mike said to Susan, "My mind feels so empty right now. Tell me something, anything, of substance that can fill it.

Whenever you tell me your thoughts my mind gets filled with other thoughts, feelings and emotions."

Susan replied, "When something comes to my mind, I will tell you." So, they just sat there sipping their coffee saying nothing. And yet, they were comfortable with each other. Only between good, close friends is it possible to sit in silence, and still feel comfortable.

It was a beautiful, quiet summer day. A wind gust broke the trance they seemed to be in. Susan thought to herself, *It's possible for one person to be unable to tell another that he or she loves the other, because of the fear of rejection. They are afraid that the other person will not accept this love. It can be very painful. So, it is easier to keep the feeling to them self.* She didn't tell this thought to Mike though, because she didn't want to endanger their relationship.

Mike told Susan about his vision, and asked her what she thought, and she said, "That is truly a mystery. Perhaps it is your future and you will meet this girl in your vision and be happy with her." Susan helped Mike believe that someday this vision could come true. Susan was glad to help Mike, but she realized that if this vision were to come true she would lose him. But, she is Mike's best friend, and she should act like it.

CHAPTER 25

Nicole was unable to sleep all night because she was thinking about her episode with Paul. She was worried about their future relationship, after they had sex. However, her anxiousness soon melted away, when Paul called and told her some good, sensitive words. This made Nicole very happy. Every girl needs some reassurance after she has sex with someone for the first time. Mostly, girls tend to want a long-term relationship, while boys tend to opt for one night stands. Only when they reach full maturity, approximately 30 years of age, do they realize that they need a family and children. Girls seem to reach maturity at a much younger age, so they are often attracted to older men.

Between 30 and 40, people try to achieve a great many goals. They feel that it is time to build their future. They feel that it will be too late, if they don't accomplish their goals during this time. This can generate a lot of fear and stress. One can worry that he or she does not fulfill his or her dreams and wishes that an unhappy future will surely follow. So, in order to avoid the stress and worry, one should try to connect with oneself so that he or she can get a feeling about the path being followed. This feeling will point you in the right direction.

If a person has followed the right path, he or she can relax and enjoy life from 40 to 50 years of age. That person has found a degree of balance and harmony. It is when he or she reaches 50 that stress and depression begin to set in. At this age, a person begins to feel that he or she must do something more as they get older, in order that he or she might live a fuller life. In cosmic terms, your life is but an instant in time, your age makes no difference.

Upon returning to reality, Nicole was very happy to hear from Paul. He asked her if she would have dinner with him and his father tonight. She told him she would like that very much. They met at an upscale Chinese restaurant called PF Changs, where they all had Chinese delicacies.

Norman (Paul's father), noticed something romantic between Paul and Nicole. To him, it appeared that they were in love, and this made Norman very happy. It was all the more reason to invest in Nicole's dream gallery. Norman told Nicole that he hired a manager who would be getting in touch with her, to help her get organized, so that the gallery would soon be ready to open its doors to the public. At long last, Nicole's dream would come to fruition.

CHAPTER 26

Mike had a couple of days yet to relax before the band's final practice, and meeting with the manager. Basically, he was all set. He just needed to make a few small changes to the music, which would not take much time, because he knew exactly what he had to do. Lisa was on his mind. Mike liked her very much. He couldn't help thinking about her mysterious hazel eyes, which made him want to know everything about her.

Mike decided to call Lisa. He couldn't call often, because of his work schedule, but when he did call her, it was as if she were waiting for him to call, and was always ready to see him. When they talked, they told each other that they missed each other. After engaging in a small conversation, they decided to have dinner together. Pizza sounded good to them both. Lisa suggested a small pizzeria which was her favorite. After dinner, they went to Mike's apartment.

Mike played the piano and sang for Lisa. For Mike, it was good practice before the band meeting. His music touched Lisa deeply and she knew that she was in love with Mike. When Mike stopped singing he felt a very strong and warm feeling for Lisa. He passionately kissed Lisa, and they made love. They were so happy and relaxed, that they fell asleep. In the morning, Mike made coffee, like he usually did when Lisa spent the night, but he also made her breakfast in bed. It was eggs, orange juice, toast and cream cheese. Lisa was so surprised because Mike always made only coffee when he woke up.

CHAPTER 27

Paul called Nicole and told her that his father hired a business manager for the gallery. He said he knew this, because he had heard his father talking on the phone. Nicole was very excited and happy to hear this news. In fact, she was ecstatic. She felt that her wishes and dreams were about to come true. She thanked Paul for all he did, and asked him if there was anything she could do for him. Paul said that the only thing that he wanted was for her to have dinner with him. She said, "It's a date." They had dinner at a well known steak house, where they both ate prime rib. After dinner, they went to Paul's apartment, and he began kissing her all over. They had unbelievable sex, which left them both feeling very tired, but very happy.

A couple of days later Norman called Nicole and asked her to meet with him and the new manager. This invitation made Nicole so happy, that she could not decide what to wear. She didn't have much time before the meeting, so she chose a business suit, a nice shirt and silver jewelry. She looked very sharp, beautiful and professional. This put her in a good mood and she believed the meeting would go quite well.

Nicole, Paul, his father and the new manager (Larry), met at a Chinese restaurant. Larry and Nicole enjoyed each other's company very much. Nicole thought that Larry was very good looking and very well mannered, and Larry thought that Nicole was also good looking, talented and intelligent. Larry told Nicole of his plans and preparations for the gallery opening. He wanted to come to Nicole's studio, take photos of the paintings, which he would then put in his computer, so that he could formulate the layout of the gallery. Nicole was very excited that work was actually being started for this project.

Paul's father gave the new manager all the rights to coordinate the business with Nicole, so that the gallery would be organized and prepared for its opening. The new manager Larry phoned Nicole and asked her for directions to her apartment. This was on a moment's notice, so Nicole quickly took a shower and began to clean her apartment. The biggest mess was in her studio, so that is where she spent most of her time cleaning. Larry arrived shortly afterward, since it was a short distance between her apartment and his office. He told Nicole that he would briefly like to see her studio and paintings. Upon seeing them, he became quite excited, because he could see that the gallery had a great future. Larry told Nicole that he would come again tomorrow at 10am to take pictures, discuss and write a plan for the opening.

The next day, Larry arrived at Nicole's apartment at exactly 10am which was a very good sign. Nicole liked punctuality. To her that was a very good characteristic. She didn't like waiting. They found a spot in the studio where they could write the plan. It was a comfortable space, with two chairs and a small table. Nicole asked Larry if he would like a cup of coffee, and he said that would be good. Nicole brought him coffee and apple cake. Larry liked the cake so much that he said "This is delicious." He told Nicole that she baked as well as she painted. She thanked him, and told him that somebody gave her the recipe, and that it was very simple and easy to make.

She said "It only takes 2 cups of sugar, 2 cups of flour, 6 eggs and a dash of salt. Mix them all together and cover it with sliced apples and cinnamon. Bake it 30 minutes at 400 degrees."

After eating the cake, and washing it down with the coffee, Larry asked Nicole to tell him about herself and her life, because he said knowing this would help them to do business together. She told him that she came from a small town in Michigan, where she grew up and attended a community college. After college she went to painting school. After that, she moved to New York, because it has a large artistic community.

Then, Larry asked Nicole when she began to paint. She said that her grandmother told her that she started painting and drawing when she was two years old. They weren't paintings per se, but just lines, ovals and spirals of different colors on paper. "Now," Larry said, "we can tell everyone that this was the beginning of your creativity and your future."

In turn, Nicole asked Larry to tell her a bit about his life. He said that he grew up in a small town in Tennessee, and went to the University of Tennessee, where he graduated with a degree in business. Now, he is working for a large advertising firm, and part time for Norman. He told Nicole that he was very glad to get this job with Norman, because he liked the arts very much and would be extremely happy to work on this project. He was also very pleased to work with such a beautiful and talented girl as herself, and he told her that he really liked her paintings. Larry said, that he was sure that they would have a great time working together.

After engaging in small conversation with Nicole about their lives, Larry said, "Now, let's get to work." So, they went to her studio which was already organized by themes, in the abstractionist style, such as geometric shapes of different colors, fountains and water, mountains and religion. Larry began taking photos of all the paintings at different angles. Later, he would choose which were the best pictures of the paintings for the gallery. Nicole followed him from behind and watched. After he had taken all the pictures that he needed, he told Nicole that he would put them in his computer, and organize them so that he could get an idea of what the gallery would look like. After that, you, Norman and I will meet and see what he thinks.

CHAPTER 28

Mike woke up early. He didn't sleep well because he was preoccupied with the final band practice and the meeting with the manager. The manager would decide if they were, or were not ready for the festival. Mike made all necessary changes to the music and songs, but he was worried that if the manager would not like something there would be no time left to do any more changing.

He made himself presentable by taking a shower, shaving and putting on fresh clothes and new jeans. On his way to the meeting, he stopped at Dunkin Donuts, for a cup of coffee, and a strawberry filled doughnut. When Mike arrived, everyone was already there. They greeted each other, and had small conversation. After that, the band began to play, and Mike began to sing song after song. The practice took two hours all together. The manager listened with all his attention, but you could not tell what he was thinking by the look on his face. One hour later, the manager told them that everything sounded very good, and they should win the competition. "Good job!" he told Mike. "I really like how you are singing - you have a very good voice." He told them to take an hour break for lunch. They went to a local delicatessen and had something very good and filling.

They went back to the studio and played for another hour, after which the manager told them that they sounded extremely good, and that they did a fantastic job. This got everybody so excited that they began to scream and give high fives to each other. The manager said, "Now you are ready for Friday night. Everybody take a couple of days off and relax, so that you are all in good shape, have plenty of rest and will be in a good mood. I want you all to be at your best. I'll see you all at the festival, and I want you to know that I am proud of you." At 5 o'clock they all split up and went their separate ways.

Mike went to his car and called Susan. He didn't want to call Lisa, because sex and emotions were not what he needed right now. He just wanted to take it easy. Susan was very happy to hear from him. Mike said to Susan, "Hi! I'd like to see you now if you have the time."

"Sure", said Susan. "I'm on my way home right now. It's been a long day. I had a lot of seminars and classes today. It left me very tired, but I'll be happy to meet you and relax a bit."

"Can we meet in our favorite coffee shop?" asked Mike. "I'd really like to relax too, and sit outside." They met each other about a half an hour later. They hugged and kissed each other and found a comfortable spot on the patio.

Mike said, "Man, is it good to sit outside here with you. When we're together here, I feel very close to you." Then, he told her about the meeting between the manager and the band, and that the manager said they sounded really good. He told Susan that he hoped to see her, with her friends and students at the festival.

Then, he asked Susan, "How was your day today?" She said she had philosophy classes, of course, and today they dealt with Plato and deductive reasoning. It was a question and answer method he used with various people to help them arrive at logical conclusions. By using this method, he could get a person to see something in a different manner, than he did originally. "That's very interesting," said Mike. "By using this method, you can help somebody understand something better and more clearly, as well as better understand themselves."

Then, Mike asked Susan, "Do you like living alone, with no boyfriend?"

Susan said, "No. It's especially difficult on holidays, when friends and family get together. It's then that I feel very lonely. Everybody seems to have a husband or boyfriend. But, I haven't met my soul mate yet, and I don't want to have just anybody. I'd rather be in a relationship that is special to me. So, I'm all alone, and I wish it wasn't that way."

Mike said, "I can really relate to that. I'm in the same situation. I haven't met someone special to me yet either. But,

I have the feeling that the girl in my vision can be that someone special for me."

Susan smiled at Mike, but at the same time she wanted him to be her someone special. However, she also realized that her someone special had to have the same feelings and emotions about her, as she did about him, and Mike did not. She was glad to have his friendship, and wanted to keep it. This was wise. She knew that she would meet her true soul mate in the future.

"Tell me Susan, what other things did you discuss with your students?" asked Mike.

To that, Susan answered, "That's a big question. We talk about many things, but one thing that comes to mind is something we talked of a few days ago, which was the purpose of our existence. We pondered why some people are creative in the arts, and most are not. Are our lives programmed? Is there such a thing as destiny or fate? If so, who or what determines our programs? If you were to ask an artist, musician or writer why they do what they do, most of them will answer that they do not know why, they just feel that they must do it, because that is all they were meant to do. However, they do get a great deal of enjoyment from it."

Mike then asked, "Is it possible to change your destiny or fate?"

Susan replied, "Destiny or fate cannot be changed. However, if one is strong, he or she can control his or her thoughts, wishes and emotions which can reduce or increase the strength of its outcome. If we can understand our actions, or why something is happening to us, then we can positively channel our emotions, so that we can be truly happy. We are creatures of free will, and we can choose right from wrong. If we choose the right way, we can be happy and comfortable. Free will is one of our greatest gifts from God."

CHAPTER 29

Nicole was daydreaming about the gallery, love and other things important to her, when the phone rang. It was Paul. She was hoping it was Larry, because she really liked the man, and couldn't wait to begin working with him. Paul asked Nicole if they could have dinner together. Nicole didn't have any plans, so she told Paul that she would be glad to. He asked her where she would like to eat, and she said she felt like Mexican.

They had a good dinner, and enjoyed spending time with each other. Nicole told Paul about her meeting with Larry, the conversation they had about their respective life stories and the pictures he took of her paintings. She also told him that Larry planned to organize the paintings by themes, put them in his computer, and show Norman the virtual gallery. She invited Paul to see it when she met with them. Paul told her that it would be very interesting for him to see this, because he loved Nicole, and everything that had to do with her happiness and her well being concerned him.

The next afternoon the phone rang, and Nicole quickly answered it. She had the feeling that Larry would call, and she was right. Nicole had good intuition. It gave her the ability to know what was happening around her. Larry told her that Norman would like to have a meeting on Monday to discuss the gallery opening, and afterwards they would go out to dinner. This made Nicole very happy.

On Monday, Nicole, Paul, Larry and Norman, met in Norman's office. Larry told Norman what he saw in Nicole's studio, and that she had an enormous amount of talent. He said he liked all the paintings and constructed a virtual gallery on his computer. He showed this to everyone and they were astonished. It was amazing. They all waited for Norman's opinion, because the future of the gallery depended upon it. The entire office was in dead silence in anticipation. After a brief pause, Norman loudly said, "This is great! Let's do this. It will be amazing!"

Everybody was happy and excited about this project. Norman said it would be a lot of work, but it would be very enjoyable and profitable. Larry said that he was really going to enjoy working with everyone on this project. Norman asked Paul to help Larry with all the financial aspects. Norman's office was in a building, which had a big hall. He rented it to other companies for exhibitions. He thought it would be perfect for the gallery. "Right now, I can imagine how it will be," he said. "Music playing softly, and people stopping in front of each picture, and talking to each other about their feelings and emotions."

Nicole said that when she went to a gallery, she would be drawn to a particular picture like a magnet. She would just stay in front of it and stare at it, to try to understand why this picture was painted, and why the artist felt that it was important and necessary. The mysterious part is that if you asked the artist why he or she felt it had to be painted, they would not be able to answer. They could only tell you that painting this picture made them very happy, like a woman feels when she gives birth to a child. They painted it because they felt a need to paint it, like it was a demand from God.

CHAPTER 30

The time was upon Mike and the band for the pop festival. It was to be tomorrow. So, Mike went to bed early, to get plenty of rest and be in good spirits. He woke up early the next morning and made some coffee, and had eggs and toast. Afterwards, he turned on the TV and watched the headlines on CNN. He watched the news until he had to leave for lunch with the other band members, and the manager. They had lunch at a Denny's restaurant at 2pm. They were all very excited about the Pop festival, which was at 4pm.

The festival was held outside in Central Park. It was very busy and overflowing with people. When Mike and the band arrived, people rushed to them, and security had to hold them back. There are things that never change at pop festivals. It seems like everywhere you look there are temporary kiosks selling food, drinks and souvenirs, and people kicking back, listening to music and mingling.

Susan came with her students, and they were loud and rowdy. Meanwhile, Paul asked Nicole to go to the festival with him. She brought her best friend Annette, who also brought a bunch of other friends too. Mike invited Lisa, who came with her friends also. At 4pm the festival officially started. It was opened by famous artists. They greeted the crowd, and told them the bands that would be performing. After they mentioned the name of each band, the crowd screamed and applauded. Mike's band was called Speed of Light and they were 5th in the line-up.

The first band started to play, and the audience began to scream and make all kinds of noise. The atmosphere was very conducive to forgetting life in the commonplace world. The people were just happy to be there. By the time the Speed of Light was ready to play, the crowd was ecstatic. People remembered this band from the last festival, and they really liked them.

Amongst the crowd were Lisa, Susan and Nicole, but they didn't know each other. When the Speed of Light took the stage, Lisa felt a huge sense of pride for Mike. She was in love with him, and she was sure that the feeling was reciprocal. However, a younger man can never be sure that he is in love. After he has sex with a girl, he can still have the same feelings of love for her, or he can begin to feel differently toward her. If his attitude about her changes, it was lust, not love. Then, he could be attracted to another pretty girl. This could happen one girl after another, until he came upon one who made him feel different. Then he realizes..... Yes! This is the only girl I need for the rest of my life! Only rarely, does a case of love at first sight occur, and if this happens, that couple is very lucky.

So, even though Lisa had strong feelings of love to Mike, he didn't feel the same way. He really liked her because they had a good time together, and great sex, but he never thought of it as a lifetime commitment. Susan had the same feelings as Lisa, and she got very excited when Mike began to sing. However, she knew that Mike didn't have the same feelings for her, and that he couldn't be her soul mate because of this. She told herself that he just liked her as his best friend, and this made her feel somewhat down. Susan realized that it was very difficult to find one's soul mate, or true love, but a person's chances are better now with the internet. Because of this, Susan was sure she would find the right person for her.

Nicole came to the festival with Paul, and when she saw Mike on the stage, she was awestruck. It was the same boy she saw at the last festival but he was also the same person she always saw in her vision. She didn't know his name, but she felt as if she had known him for a long, long time. Because of this, she realized that she really didn't love Paul. All her thoughts and feelings were centered around Mike. Nicole thought that Mike could be her soul mate. She had feelings of true love for him. This was a turning point in her relationship with Paul. She just wanted to be his friend now.

Mike sang really well....with all his heart. The fans

adored him and screamed. After the band finished playing, the manager told them that security would help them get to their bus. Fans rushed towards them to get their autographs, and journalists took pictures and asked questions. One journalist asked Mike, "Are you married?"

Mike answered, "Not at the moment, but I'm sure I will be in the future. I'm not ready yet, but someday I want to have a wife and children." After they answered some questions, and gave some autographs, security surrounded them and escorted them to the bus.

The band and the manager went to a restaurant for a bite to eat. When they sat down, the manager said, "Wow! It was a great day. You guys did a fantastic job. I'm proud of you all. Soon, we will have a contract with a promoter to tour the country. In the future, I hope to travel the world." This made everybody so happy that they slapped each other on the back and gave high fives. Next, the manager told them, "Since we made decent money at this festival, I want you all to take a month long vacation and relax, because we have to be prepared for a country wide tour, which involves a lot of hard work. I will be in touch with all of you during the next month. I'm sure that we'll have a great future, and I wish everybody, Good Luck!"

CHAPTER 31

Norman told Larry that he needed a name for the new business and a written business plan for running the gallery. Larry asked Paul to help him with the financial aspects of the business, because Paul had a financial education. So, after they diligently worked together, they called the business of the gallery "Nicole's View Thru Painting," formulated a business plan for it, and showed it to Norman. He replied, "Good job fellas. You've worked very hard and fast. I like it a lot. I'll see you both in my office this afternoon, and bring that beautiful girl Nicole with you."

Nicole couldn't sleep the night after the festival, because Mike, the male singer at the festival looked exactly like the man in her vision, and she could think of nothing else. Nicole felt that she might be in love with this man. However, she also thought that this couldn't be possible, because she had never talked to him, and knew nothing about him. This was all she could think about all night.

In the morning, Larry called. He told her that they would all be meeting with Norman in the afternoon. He also told her that he and Paul made a business plan that he would show Norman, and that he was sure that she would find it interesting too. This jolted Nicole back to reality. She took a shower, put on her make-up, got dressed and went out. When Nicole arrived at Norman's office, everyone was already there, loudly discussing the business plan, but everyone's attention shifted to Nicole when she entered the office. They were all glad to see her, because they all liked her, especially Paul, who was in love with her. She was the best woman he had ever met in his entire life.

They all sat down at a round table. Norman said that the business plan of Nicole's View Thru Painting was finished, and it was excellent. He said that Larry and Paul did a very good job on it. Norman told them that in order to follow the business plan, some employees need to be hired for maintenance. The hall needed to be cleaned and prepared for painting. He put his trust in Larry to hire some painters and choose the colors. He said that, "After the hall is readied, a more difficult job lies ahead." Norman told Larry that he will need to bring the paintings from Nicole's apartment, and get them organized and hung on the walls. He also told Larry to coordinate the advertising in newspapers, TV, radio and online. When everything is all set up, we will begin selling tickets online, and at the ticket window of the building. "I want a colorful sign above the ticket window saying 'Nicole's View Thru Painting.' We will sell tickets every day, so we must hire a cashier and a cleaning person. Larry, hire an assistant manager to help you with the advertising. I have a feeling that this business will be very successful." Everybody was very excited about this business and its grand opening.

Nicole and Paul left, while Larry and Norman stayed in the office to further discuss details of the business. Paul asked Nicole to have dinner with him, and Nicole agreed. They decided they wanted something simple, so they both had grilled chicken sandwiches and sodas. Nicole didn't want a fancy dinner with Paul, because her feelings had changed toward him. She regarded Paul as more of a friend, than a lover. Nicole realized that her heart and soul now belonged to the person with blue eyes from her vision. She knew that it was the same singer she saw at the festival. They spoke a great deal to each other about the gallery opening, but Paul noticed that something was different. Something had changed between them. Paul asked Nicole if she would like to finish their conversation at her apartment, but she told him that she was very tired, and just wanted to go home and rest.

When Nicole got to her apartment and studio, she was just happy to be around her paintings. She began to paint, but had no idea what she was painting. She was very relaxed and thought about nothing. Nicole began to hear music, and had the vision of the same person she saw singing at the festival. She started to paint, but had no idea what she was painting. It was as if her hands were guided unconsciously by her brain. It was a truly creative moment, and it made Nicole extremely happy. When she finished, she gazed upon the picture, and it was a blend of waves and lines of different colors - abstractionism!

After painting, she felt like calling her mother. Her mother asked her all kinds of questions about things which Nicole didn't want to talk about. Nicole's mother never understood her anyway, and she wondered why she even bothered to call her. Nicole and her mother didn't share the same view of happiness, love and life. Unlike some mothers and daughters who are very close to each other, Nicole and her mother were diametrically opposed to each other. They could not share their feelings, emotions and secrets with each other. Nicole thought to herself, *My mother and I have two different personalities. I don't expect any understanding between us. I just love her, because she is my mother.* Nicole remembered one of the things that her mother told her. "Love your life, and the people around you. The more love you give, the greater amount you will receive." After talking with her mother, and answering her usual questions, Nicole went to bed, thought about the gallery and once again had the vision in which she heard music and saw the man with blue eyes.

Larry hired two men to clean and paint the hall. They told Larry that it would probably take about two weeks. Larry also hired an assistant manager. Larry called his friend Aaron, and asked him if he would come to Norman's office for an interview. Aaron showed up at Norman's office at 4pm. He was tall, handsome and in very good shape, 35 years old, well educated with a degree in history, and he loved computers. He had a lot of knowledge about television and newspapers because at one time, he ran an advertising business with Larry. When Larry asked him to be the assistant manager for this project, Aaron found the idea quite intriguing and very interesting. Norman asked Aaron some questions about his education, what kinds of art he liked and about his experience in advertising. Norman liked this man and said, "Welcome to our project."

Larry and Aaron both contacted TV and radio stations, newspapers, and other forms of advertising such as freeway billboards etc.. Aaron devoted a lot of time to building a website and advertising on the internet through facebook and twitter. They planned to be finished in about one month. It probably could have been done sooner, but Aaron was only working part-time with Larry because he was working full time for a large advertising firm.

Aaron told Norman, that he was very excited about the pictures that he saw on Larry's computer, and that he wanted to meet with Nicole, to better understand her personality. He needed to know her likes, dislikes, feelings and emotions before advertising. They decided that tomorrow, at the same time, they would meet. This was a good time for Aaron, because he was off from his full time job. Larry phoned Paul, and asked him to bring Nicole to the meeting tomorrow at 4pm. Nicole was very glad to be asked to this meeting, because she was ready to do anything necessary for the gallery opening.

Nicole called Annette, and asked her if she would like to go shopping with her. Nicole wanted some new clothes, jewelry and shoes, to have a really great look for the meeting tomorrow. They met at the mall, and as usual, Annette was as fresh as spring time and smiling. They found everything they wanted, and they talked and laughed as they went through the mall. Annette enjoyed Nicole's company. After shopping they went to a small coffee shop in the mall, where they relaxed and did some people watching. They both ordered mango juice and chocolate cake with whipped cream and cherries on the top. It was Nicole's favorite cake.

Nicole asked Annette about her relationship with her boyfriend, and Annette answered, "Nothing has changed. Everything's still the same. He's a good person, but I just look upon him as a friend. I don't see a future with him, so I don't have any serious plans."

Nicole said, "I'm sure you'll meet someone special."

Annette laughed and said, "I'm too busy right now with my work at the boutique to even think about it. I can only think about enjoying myself and life at the moment. I have a few years yet before I have to start thinking about marriage."

Nicole told Annette about the man who sang at the festival and how he was just like the man in her dreams and vision. Annette remembered him and said that he was very good. She said that she understood why Nicole dreamt about him. Nicole also told her about the new gallery opening and that she had a business meeting tomorrow about it. Annette wished her good luck, and the two departed and went their separate ways.

The next day, at 4pm, Nicole arrived at Norman's office in new clothes and jewelry for the business meeting. Everyone was already there. Aaron, the assistant manager, was shocked to see that Nicole looked so beautiful, and he found it very exciting to work in this business with her. He began to ask her a battery of questions, which seemed eerily similar to a psychological evaluation. He asked Nicole about her education, her dreams and goals, what she watched on TV, the type of music she liked, what she liked to eat, etc. After Nicole answered Aaron's questions, he found that she had a very interesting personality, and she was able to relay her thoughts and feelings on canvas.

Aaron told Nicole that he now could operate the business in the best possible way because he had a true picture of her personality. He told her that he would be looking at all the pictures in Larry's computer, so that he could do the best possible advertising for the business. Aaron then went home, spent a few hours by the computer, and looked at Nicole's paintings. Afterwards, he was very excited and thought to himself, *Yes, these pictures can bring a lot of money to this business.*

CHAPTER 32

In the morning, Mike woke up with the realization that he was free for the entire month, and that he had enough money to relax and do whatever he wanted. These thoughts put him in a very good mood. He decided to just lay around and relax for a while. During this relaxation period, he thought it would be good to go somewhere on a vacation. He wanted to take Lisa with him, so he called her and said that he had some vacation time, and wanted her to go away with him for a couple of weeks. Lisa said that she had to talk to her boss, but otherwise, she would be happy to go with him. She said, "I'll call you back and let you know."

Mike liked a warm climate, and desired to live somewhere in the south, where there was no snow or cold weather. He really fancied the idea of going on a vacation to Hawaii. There, he could relax for a couple of weeks. He and Lisa could stay at a good hotel on the beach, which had a high class restaurant, and a night club where they could dance. He just wanted to have a romantic time with Lisa. Mike had been to Hawaii before with his parents, and had a great time. The weather was always wonderful, and the water was warm, just like bath water. Lisa had never been to Hawaii, but she had heard nothing but good things about it, through friends and relatives. Mike found a very good deal on the flight and hotel on the internet. He booked it for two people, one week before they were to leave. Mike asked Lisa to spend the rest of the day and the night with him. All that time, they talked and dreamed about this vacation.

Mike decided to call Susan because he hadn't seen her for a while. When he called her, she didn't answer, so he left a message. A couple of hours went by and she still hadn't returned his call, so he began to worry. This was unusual to Mike, because he was never concerned about other people. To him, everybody had their own lives. Mike called her one more time, and Susan finally picked up the phone. She had just come home and was very tired, but when she heard Mike's voice, it filled her with energy. They had a short conversation, and decided to meet at their usual hangout, the coffee shop at 5pm.

They met at exactly 5 o'clock, found a good place to sit, and ordered coffee and cheesecake. Mike asked Susan, "I haven't seen you for a while, so tell me what's new and exciting in your life?"

Susan said, "Same old, same old." She told him that she spent some time at home, but most of her time at the university. Her students were constantly surprising her with their thoughts and feelings. For example, one of her students told her of a repeating dream he had been having. The dream is of his future, where he is older, married and with several kids. He can clearly see his home in great detail, like the colors of the walls, the type of furniture and his children. He also sees himself in an office, writing about different cultures in other countries. This dream repeated itself every night.

Susan said that this presented a puzzle to her. He lives in the present, dreams of his future, but never talks about his past. Every day he tells a new story about what he dreamed of his future life. But, today he spoke of dreaming about his future life with his wife and children. He saw himself in his office, writing about Japanese culture. The people worked a lot of hours, and every Friday they would get together with co-workers for dinner and karaoke. People were very friendly, and they kept a special room in their homes, filled with different forms of entertainment for the children. This gave him the thought that it would be a good thing to have for his children. It would be a good training ground for patience and societal adaptation.

"That is a very interesting scenario, indeed," said Mike. "It'll even be more interesting if these things really happen in the future, and if they do, I wonder if he will remember them happening in his dream?" Susan said that she would be keeping in touch with him to see if these things actually occurred.

Then, Mike and Susan talked about the latest movies

that were now showing, and other things that were going on in the world. Afterwards, he told her that he was going on vacation and would get in touch with her when he returned. Susan didn't know that he was taking Lisa with him, so she was just a bit envious that he was going on vacation, and they departed as good friends.

CHAPTER 33

The idea of a vacation made Mike feel very refreshed and invigorated. It was a feeling that everybody felt before they went on a vacation. He began to think of the things he must do in preparation for this event. He made a list of the things he had to buy and what needed to be done. The list was quite long, and he realized that many things had to be done prior to leaving. He had to make a lot of phone calls, and do a lot of shopping and packing. Early the next morning, he made the necessary phone calls, and confirmed the flight and hotel. He called Lisa, and made arrangements to go shopping together and buy everything that they wanted and might need.

Mike liked Lisa's choice of clothes and was glad that he asked her to go with him. He was happy that she would be his girl on the vacation. He wanted to see her choice of beachwear, dining wear and clothes she would wear just to go out. Mike also had very good taste in clothes and food. He was excited to have Lisa with him because she looked beautiful, and he was the kind of man who liked it when other men looked at her, and were envious of him. At such a moment, he would be extremely happy that the woman was with him, and Lisa was the kind of woman who grabbed the attention of other men. So, Mike was happy entertaining these thoughts when he met her in the mall.

They spent all day shopping, choosing clothes, novelties and accessories, shoes and luggage. After shopping, they just needed to pack, but they were also very tired from shopping, so they decided to relax for a while in a small café in the mall. They ordered sandwiches and sodas. The shopping excursion gave them a big appetite and they ate very fast. While they were in the café, Lisa told Mike that her boss gave her two weeks' vacation time. They both felt very good about this, but getting prepared was also a lot of hard work, and yet it was exciting. Even though it was strenuous and tedious, it was well worth it, because a vacation is like a dream come true.

Mike asked Lisa to spend the night with him at his apartment, and she was glad to get this invitation, because Lisa usually waited for a while to get a call from Mike. He told her that he thought about her, but he could only call when he had free time, since he was always very busy. Actually, Mike was never preoccupied with any woman. He just wanted to live his own life, and he only thought about Lisa or Susan occasionally. However, the woman in his vision was always on his mind. She, and the vision, touched him deeply. They were very special to him.

Lisa went with Mike to his apartment, where they watched some TV for a while before Mike played a CD of romantic music, and during that time, they held and kissed each other. Mike felt very comfortable with Lisa, and he really enjoyed this moment. It was a very romantic evening. In the morning, Mike made coffee as usual. Lisa had coffee and a cheese Danish, and left for work. Mike spent the morning playing the piano. There was just something on his mind that he couldn't remember. There was something mysterious tugging at his inner being. And then, he had the vision of the beautiful girl with all the colorful paintings flying behind her.

Another person would find it very difficult to understand how he could be making love to Lisa, have meetings with Susan at the coffee shop and still have visions of another girl. One might say that Mike suffers from a sexual disorder, and that he has a lot of sexual confusion. However, nobody can judge others, only a higher power can pass judgment. To do so will only bring negativity into one's life. Everybody should strive to improve his or her self confidence and well being by respecting others. As long as another person's feelings or emotions do not have a bad or dangerous effect on others, then that is their business. Just let them follow their own path. Tolerance, respect, love and understanding are the keys to living a life of fulfillment.

CHAPTER 34

Paul phoned Nicole and told her that he missed their private relationship. The only time he seemed to be able to see her was at his father's office for business meetings. He told her he missed her and wanted to see her outside of the business sphere. Nicole told him that she was also tired of business talk all the time, and missed her creative moments and their romantic meetings. Paul was very happy to hear this, and they agreed to meet at a restaurant known for its home-style cooking. At the restaurant, they still found themselves talking about the gallery and its opening. However, they were just happy to be alone with each other. After eating, they went to Nicole's apartment and had a very romantic time. It was then that Nicole, even though she liked Paul, began to regard him more of a friend, because her soul was beginning to long for the singer at the Pop festival.

Aaron spent a few days just looking at Nicole's paintings and thinking about them. The more he thought about them, the more he enjoyed looking at them. He called Nicole and told her about his feelings for them. At this time, Aaron wasn't married, and didn't have a girlfriend. Aaron met with Paul in Norman's office, and asked him about Nicole. Paul told him that she is a wonderful girl, and that they sometimes see each other. Aaron asked Paul to find out if Nicole had an unattached girlfriend, so that they could go double dating. They might go out to eat and do some other fun things. Paul said it sounded like a good idea, and that he would talk to Nicole.

The next day, Paul called Nicole and told her that Aaron asked him for a favor. He told her that Aaron wanted him to ask her if she had a girlfriend who would be willing to go out with him on a double date with them. Nicole also thought that it was a good idea, and told Paul of Annette. Nicole told Paul that Annette has a boyfriend, but it was nothing serious. She told him that Annette was looking for someone special, someone who could be her soul-mate. Nicole told Paul that she wanted to help Annette be happy. Paul told Nicole that he would talk to Aaron about it, and they would decide when the best day and time to do this would be. After speaking with Paul, Nicole called Annette, and asked her if she would be willing to do this. She told her that Aaron was very handsome, and the new assistant manager of the gallery. Annette was very excited about this. Nicole said that she would wait for Paul to call back, and let her know all the details. The following morning, Paul called Nicole and told her that Aaron would like to go out next Friday, and that he would pay for everyone's dinner. Nicole called Annette and relayed this information to her. Annette was thrilled about this, but also very nervous. She had a very good feeling about this meeting, and so many thoughts were racing through her mind, that she had trouble sleeping.

Friday morning Paul called Nicole, and told her that they would all meet at her apartment at 5pm, and from there they would all go to an establishment where they could eat, listen to music and dance. Nicole called Annette and relayed this.

At 5pm. Friday, they all met at Nicole's, and from the first moment, Aaron liked Annette, and she liked him. After exchanging niceties, they departed for the nightclub. There, Annette talked to Aaron a lot, and smiled at him often. You could tell she wanted his attention. They ordered a wonderful dinner, and when the music turned romantic, Aaron asked Annette to slow dance with him. While they danced together, they forgot about everything and everybody else, and just got lost in their feelings for each other. They had a good connection and were happy at this moment. After they danced, they returned to the table, and everyone enjoyed dinner. After this, Aaron told Annette that he would like to see her again, and asked her for her phone number and email address. Annette was so glad he asked.

The next day Annette called Nicole and told her that Aaron asked for her phone number and email address. Nicole said that's a good sign, because she thought that Aaron was a very good man. She said, "He is handsome, intelligent, courteous and well mannered." Normally, Annette called Nicole every once in a while, but today she called her 4 times, to talk about Aaron. It was as if he was all she could think about. Nicole got tired of talking about Aaron, but was also understanding. It's normal for a woman to talk about a man all the time if she has an interest in him. Out of friendship, she tried to give Annette all the understanding and support she could.

Nicole and Annette met each other at painting school, where they studied all types of different painting styles. After painting school however, they went in different directions. Nicole continued to paint, while Annette became a clothing designer, but they remained friends. They both differed in looks and character. Annette was blonde, with dark brown eyes and a great figure. She sort of resembled a Barbie doll. She was very energetic and outgoing, and always knew what to say at any given moment, in any conversation. There were a lot of conversations too, as she was always surrounded by men. She was always smiling, and was very easy to communicate and get along with. Nicole, on the other hand, was a romantic and a dreamer. She didn't like being around a lot of people, preferring to be around true friends. She was very critical, unsure of herself, and very analytical of everything that occurred in her life. But, aside from their differences, they still liked each other and remained good friends.

Aaron called Annette a week after they had met. Annette began to worry that he hadn't called earlier. Usually, men called her constantly, and she would choose which ones to go out with. It never concerned her. However, she found herself worrying that he had not called her. This feeling was new to her, but she liked it. So, Annette was elated that he called. She forgot about her boyfriend, and all the other men who called her. She only had Aaron on her mind. It was as if she had entered another dimension. She became much more romantic. She didn't care to go shopping all the time, or talk on the phone with her girlfriends about unimportant things. This meant nothing to her anymore. She only wanted to talk to Aaron, and to Nicole about Aaron. Annette wondered how this could be. She only met him one time, and everything changed. It was like she was a completely different person. She thought to herself, *could this be true love*?

Upon answering Aaron's call, she was quite nervous talking with him. Her throat became very dry and she started to lose her voice. She asked Aaron to wait a moment while she took a drink of water. When they resumed their conversation, her face turned red and her heart started to beat very fast. Her emotions gave her trouble understanding what he said. She felt so stupid. She acted as if something else caused her not to hear what he said. She asked him to repeat it. He said that he was so excited from their meeting that he wanted to call her right away, but wasn't able to. His other two jobs kept him so busy that he couldn't find the time, but she was always on his mind, and that he was glad they were able to talk now, and that he was happy to hear her voice. He asked her if they could meet next Saturday and spend some time together. Annette said "Most definitely". He asked her to think about where she would like to go and what she would like to do. He said he would call her next Saturday morning and find out. Annette replied "Sounds good. I'll wait for your call." She was so affected by his call that she couldn't find anything else to say. Aaron said, "Bye, and have a good day", and hung up.

After Aaron had hung up, Annette just sat gazing at the wall. It was like time had stopped, and she was in another world. When she finally returned to reality, she found herself sitting in a chair with the phone still in her hands, making the sound that it does when it is off the hook for a period of time. She never had such feelings and emotions before. In time, she cooled down, relaxed and returned to normal. The phone rang and she answered it. It was one of the men who called her all the time. He wanted to meet with her, but she told him she couldn't because she was very busy.

The next morning, she woke up in a very good mood. It was three days before Saturday, and she was already thinking of what clothes and jewelry she would wear. After breakfast, she left for work at the designing boutique. It was a good paying job, so she could afford many of the finer things in life. It was a very busy day with a great deal of customers.

CHAPTER 35

As the Romans said, Tempus Fugit, or time flies. Soon, Mike and Lisa would fly to Hawaii, where Mike would see some of the best looking women he has ever seen in his life. They were all packed and ready to leave. It was a time of great anticipation, like the feeling that one gets before a vacation, important holiday or event, such as Thanksgiving, Christmas, Independence Day, a birthday party or wedding celebration. No matter what happens, when these days arrive, it's a very exciting moment. This was the feeling that Mike had.

The next afternoon, Mike called Susan, and they arranged to meet at the coffee shop where they always met. Meeting with Susan had become a necessity for Mike, and he was sure that it was also very important for Susan. Their interactions were helpful to both of them. Susan was a very intelligent girl, and every time they met, Mike learned something new from her. His mind was opened to new horizons. Their conversations also helped Susan to see things from a new perspective. They helped her see things differently. When they met, Susan was very tired. She taught a lot of classes that day, and was glad to relax and talk with Mike.

Mike asked Susan, "What's on your mind? What're you thinking about?"

Susan answered, "Nothing in particular. I'm just lost in thought about what happened today and what I talked about." She told Mike that one of her female students asked her what she thought about monogamy and her opinion of it. Susan said, "I told her that no matter what lifestyle you have, it should feel natural to you. Your sexual relationships, the clothing you wear, etc. are of no importance, as long as you are at one with yourself and the world around you. You should have friends who have similar tastes and share your way of life. However, you have to remember that your actions cannot be offensive or dangerous to others. Those actions must be accepted in the cultural framework of the country you are in, because if you ignore the culture, it is as if you are ignoring the law. Life will become extremely unhappy for you and, everybody wants to be happy and comfortable. To ignore the culture of the country in which you reside is selfish, because you are thinking only of yourself, and people will ignore you. You will have no friends. You will be all alone. To have friends, and be a friend is very important. Sometimes, you might be very tired, watching your favorite program on TV, reading your email or be involved in a game. At the same time a friend needs your help, and you should be able to drop whatever you are doing to give your aid, and vice versa. So, how you look does not matter. What is significant is the type of person you are inside, and the quality of your emanations."

Mike said to Susan, "I really enjoy talking with you. I always get something from you, and I always feel fresh and more open minded. Why are you so smart Susan? Was your intelligence inherited?"

"Intelligence is not an inherited quality," said Susan. "My mother was very smart, but it was not from schooling. She was street smart. Her intelligence came from experience. My father was also smart. He was an attorney."

CHAPTER 36

Saturday morning, Mike and Lisa arrived at JFK airport at 8:00am for their flight to Hawaii. It was late September, raining, getting cool and the airport was quite busy. The people wanted to go to warmer destinations. Their flight wasn't until 9:42am, so they thought they'd get a bite to eat before the flight, which was to take about 6 hours. After they checked in, they went to a small breakfast nook for coffee and egg sandwiches. When they finished eating, they boarded their flight with nervous anticipation.

They landed in Oahu at 9:54am Hawaiian time. When they disembarked the plane, they immediately smiled and hugged each other. The air was warm, and the sight of palm trees and the smell of the ocean made them feel energized. They boarded a bus which was to take them to their hotel, which was on Waikiki Beach. The sky was clear, and the people were all laughing and smiling and it was about 82 degrees. "This is great! What a life! Now, this is the way to live!" Mike said to Lisa.

She said "I can't wait to get on the beach and go swimming and sunbathing. This is FANTASTIC! Thank you

Mike!"

Their hotel was right on the beachfront. Their room was on the third floor with a balcony where you could go outside, drink your morning coffee and feel the ocean breeze. They decided to unpack later. Right now they wanted to get on the beach, go swimming, feel the sand under their feet and the sun on their backs. The beach was absolutely wonderful. It was a good thing they were wearing sandals, because the sand was hot. They set up an umbrella and lawn chairs, spread beach towels on the sand and went in the water. They were shocked. The water was warm! It was like taking a bath. The water was so pleasant that they could have spent hours in it, but they would have looked like prunes when they came out. So, after about 15 minutes, they went on the beach to lay in the sun. Lisa looked great, all wet and in her string bikini. All the men on the beach were staring and glancing at her. As she always did, she caught their attention. They were all jealous that she was with Mike and he was glad she was with him.

Lisa asked Mike what he had planned for tonight. He told her that he wanted to take her to a traditional Hawaiian feast, a luau, where they slow roasted a pig underground, wrapped the meat in palm leaves, served vegetables, pineapple and coconut milk. After spending a couple of hours on the beach, they returned to their room. The atmosphere of their surroundings and being alone with each other for two weeks made them both feel sexually aroused. Mike groped her body with his hands and kissed her hard. She melted in his arms and succumbed to his every desire. He laid her down on the king size bed with satin sheets, where they had incredibly great sex. Afterwards, they just laid there, holding and kissing each other for a while, and then took a shower together.

In the mid afternoon, they rented a car from the rental agency at the hotel, and drove to the site of the luau. There, they were greeted by Hawaiian women doing hula dances and adorning them with leis. The feast site was located on a small volcanic hilltop overlooking an inlet. The water was shimmering and the sunlight was dancing on the tree leaves. The people were very upbeat and the air was festive. In about 15 minutes they would unearth the roasted pig, which had been slow cooking over coals for 24 hours. After a spectacular dinner, which took about two hours, they relaxed and watched a beautiful sunset. Lisa said, "This is the best vacation I've ever taken."

Mike smiled and said, "Wait 'til tomorrow. We're going to see something awesome."

"What?" asked Lisa.

Mike answered, "Mount Kilauea, the most active volcano in the world."

The next day, they viewed the volcano, which was truly a sight to behold. Mike told Lisa about the goddess Pele, the goddess of fire, whom the natives worshiped at one time, and they believed she lived in the volcano. And, after that, they chartered a small plane and went island hopping, to see the beauty of all the islands. Of course, every day they went swimming in the ocean and laid in the sun. This was the course of their Hawaiian vacation. Every day they went swimming, got a deeper suntan, went to native Hawaiian events and took sightseeing tours. It never rained and it was never cool. The weather was perfect.

During the second week of their vacation, they basically spent most of the time sunbathing, swimming and eating at the hotel restaurant. It became like a routine, and they started to miss the city life of New York. On the last day of their two week vacation, they went sunbathing, but didn't have anything to say to each other. After about two hours on the beach, they returned to their room and began packing for the return flight the next morning. Departing wasn't as exciting as arriving.

They boarded their return flight at 10:00am in Oahu. The flight back was not a nonstop flight but had a brief layover in Los Angeles for refueling. It was a bit cooler, but nothing like what awaited them in New York. They arrived at JFK airport at approximately 6:00pm. The weather was a far cry from that of Hawaii. It was about 52 degrees and windy. Mike got a taxi, and had the driver take Lisa to her apartment, which was on the way to Mike's apartment.

He had a great vacation with Lisa, but he began to be bored with her. He regarded her as a wonderful, sensitive girl. It's true he had great sex with her, but after awhile she began to look the same all the time. She all the time talked of stupid things, and never had anything important to say. After the taxi dropped her off, all of his attention became focused on music and his vision of the beautiful girl with the paintings behind her.

Now that Mike's vacation time was over, the band manager called him and told him that he had negotiated a new contract and needed some new songs. Mike was working hard trying to compose new music when the vision returned to him. He composed music with the fury of a man obsessed. He didn't call Lisa after this, because he felt that their relationship was over. He wasn't sure if he would ever call her again. Instead, he called Susan and told her that he really wanted to see her.

CHAPTER 37

It was a Wednesday, and Paul phoned Nicole and asked if she and Annette would like to meet at Aaron's house for a get together Friday night. Nicole said that she liked the idea and that she would get in touch with Annette and call him back. When Nicole called Annette to inform her of the invitation to this informal gathering, she was surprised that Annette was so happy to hear from her. Annette was so excited to hear this that she quickly responded, "Yes, yes. I would like to go there very much." Nicole called Paul back and told him that she and Annette would both be there and asked him for directions to his house.

Friday afternoon, Annette came to Nicole's apartment. She was already prepared for their meeting. She couldn't wait. Nicole showered, and applied her make-up. When she was clean, fresh and ready, they departed for Aaron's house, which was in a small town about 30 minutes from New York City. When they arrived, they found his house to be not too large, with trees, bushes, flowers and a well manicured lawn. Paul was already there, and greeted them. He asked them to come inside. The house was just as lovely inside as it was outside. The walls were adorned with large impressionist style pictures of nature. The living room had a fireplace, surrounded by leather furniture and a three tiered glass table. On this table were chips and dip, hors d'oeuvres and sweet snacks. It was a very cozy setting, with romantic music playing.

They relaxed on the leather furniture and Aaron served some very good white wine. Everybody nibbled on the food and talked about art, music and their favorite movies. It was a very friendly and natural setting. After drinking a few glasses of wine, they danced and watched a DVD movie about art and love. Everyone left with a very good feeling about this evening.

CHAPTER 38

It was Thursday, and the presentation to the media and dignitaries was set for Saturday at 10:00am. Larry had put a great deal of effort and time preparing the gallery for the presentation and its opening. When everything had been repaired, cleaned and painted he sent workers with a truck to pick up the paintings from Nicole's studio. Two of the workers spent a couple of days hanging the paintings according to Larry's plan. Aaron spent a lot of time arranging the advertising on TV and the radio. Together, they prepared the presentation. From Norman's budget, they procured an array of small sandwiches, fruits, sweet tidbits and beverages. Now that everything was ready for the presentation, all that was needed was one last meeting with everyone involved. As his final act before the grand opening, Larry called Nicole, Paul and Aaron about the meeting Friday, which was to be at 10:00am.

Friday morning, Norman told everybody that all aspects of the plan for the gallery went perfectly, and that they were now on the "last paragraph" before the opening. With that, he poured a glass of champagne for them and said,

"A toast of thanks. I called this meeting because I would like to express my gratitude to everyone who has made this magnificent presentation possible. I would personally like to thank each and every one of you. Thank you Larry for getting the building in top shape. It looks marvelous, and the arrangement is wonderful. Thank you Aaron for doing a fantastic job with the advertising. I like it very much. Thank you Paul for doing an excellent job with the financial aspects and most of all, I extend my utmost thanks to you Nicole, for giving us this opportunity to display your beautiful paintings. I'm sure that everyone else will love them as much as we do." They all cheered, and swallowed their champagne.

Saturday morning, everybody arrived at 9:00am, one hour prior to the presentation. They checked everything one last time to make sure that everything was ready, inside and outside. At 10:00am they opened the doors. The first guests to arrive were mainly friends, acquaintances, clients and Aaron's co-workers. He sent out a lot of invitations to relatives, friends and clients. Nicole invited her mother as well as Annette, with her friends. Journalists from newspapers, and television stations also attended. There were gentlemen dressed in black attire, offering attendees finger sandwiches and beverages. Most of the guests stayed for quite a while. They seemed to get great enjoyment from the paintings, staring at one for quite a while and then moving to another. The atmosphere was very pleasant, and everyone appeared to have a good time. It was awesome. Larry announced to the audience that he would like to introduce the central figure of this display of art - NICOLE! They all gathered around her, to talk with her and ask questions.

Annette, with her friends, wandered around and enjoyed the paintings, but the number of them astounded her. They all had different themes, and no one picture could be said to be better than another. Every painting was different, and each one transmitted Nicole's energy. They would stare at each one to get the feeling that it delivered. Sometimes, they didn't understand why they liked one painting more than another, or why it grabbed his or her attention. It was a mystery. Sometimes, we feel that we are drawn to something and want to be around it, but we don't know why. There are times when beauty can't be explained. We are just happy to view it. Nature's beauty is the same. Take, for instance, a beautiful sunset and the amount of money people spend going to scenic places, like Niagara Falls, the Grand Canyon, National Parks, the mountains or the ocean. To gaze upon such things gives us energy. This energy allows us to see things in different ways, and gives us a greater understanding of the truth and meaning of our existence.

Every day, more people from the media came to interview Nicole and take pictures. It was as if she were a national hero. The grand opening, which was in two weeks, was announced on television news and in print. It was treated as if it was something really important, and that made Nicole happy. Norman was very happy too. He was considering opening a hotel and restaurant close to the gallery. He asked Larry to reserve seats at a four star restaurant for a dinner celebration.

Norman invited some very big names to view the gallery before its grand opening. He even invited the Mayor of New York City, and some others who were high up in the political ranks. There was a lot of food, drink, delicacies and well dressed men and women. Nicole looked particularly beautiful sporting a new diamond necklace, which was a gift from Norman. It was a high class affair, and a moment of triumph for Nicole. However, she deserved the jewelry and accolades, because she put all her heart and soul into her paintings. She worked very hard for this. Any artist who did this could expect great results.

Nicole's mother arrived just prior to the public opening of the gallery, and stayed at Nicole's apartment. She always looked upon Nicole's painting as the antics of a spoiled girl. She didn't believe that Nicole took her painting so seriously. She believed that all young women should find a good man, who made decent money, get married and raise children. And now, when her mother came to the presentation, she was shocked to see all the attention that her daughter was getting. There were journalists from newspapers and magazines and interviewers from television stations all wanting to interview her. The biggest shock of all was the amount of money she was making from this. When she heard and read all the good news about Nicole, it made her feel a sense of pride. She began to give her daughter the love and respect she deserved.

Nicole was very happy about the changes in her mother's attitude. She thought that only her success could bring her mother to understand her. However, it really didn't matter to Nicole what actually caused these changes, it was more important that her mother now gave her respect, understanding and admiration. This was very important because, love, understanding and respect between children and parents brings happiness, balance, love and harmony which leads to a brighter future.

CHAPTER 39

Mike and Susan met in the same café where they always met, and were very happy to see each other. They both ordered espressos and Mike told Susan all about his trip to Hawaii, but he didn't tell her he took Lisa with him. His story sounded like heaven to her. It excited her, and she said, "I want to go to Hawaii right now."

Then Mike said, "Tell me what's new and exciting in your life." She told him that her students surprised her by asking her some profound social questions, which she could not answer immediately. She told them that she would have to do a bit of research concerning these questions, but that she would answer the questions shortly. Thus, she had to spend a lot of time in the library, and on the internet. She showed him the list of questions.

1) *What is the effect of the advertising industry on our perception of beauty?*
2) *How might feminism affect birth and abortion rates?*
3) *Is there an afterlife?*
4) *What would life be like if I weren't an American?*

5) *Will capitalism be the demise of the American economy?*

6) *Does Mother Nature respond in the same way that "God" does, via natural disasters?*

7) *Does everyone's ancestry tell the prospects of their purpose or future?*

8) *How might the pervasiveness of racism affect social construction and family ties?*

9) *How might the removal of fast food from urban communities affect obesity/diabetes rates?*

Mike was dumbfounded. He said, "I was under the delusion that younger people were only concerned with video games and social networking." Susan laughed and told Mike the answers she had arrived at via her research. They were:

1) *Advertising does not affect our perception of beauty. We already dictate what is beautiful and what is not. It is merely a tool used to promote products and items that will help us to achieve our perception of beauty.*

2) *Feminism will cause birth rates to decline, because women now have career goals just like men. To give birth would hinder a woman's career. So, if a woman does get pregnant, she will want an abortion, so that she can pursue her career. Therefore, the abortion rate will rise.*

3) *There is an afterlife, but it may be something totally different from what we are brought up to believe. A human being is basically a form of energy, and energy cannot be destroyed. It can only be transformed into another form of energy.*

4) *If I weren't American, then I would be a citizen of a country with a more oppressive government, unless I lived in Canada, the U.K. or Australia. I would be living under a ruling class. I would yearn to break the shackles of tyranny to experience more freedom. GOD BLESS AMERICA!*

5) *No! Capitalism is a basic tenet of nature, so it will not be the downfall of the American economy. Since the dawn of recorded history, man has sold items and products to make a profit.*

6) *Perhaps. Natural disasters are the ecosystem's way of responding to the wounds that man can inflict upon the earth. For instance, deforestation can lead to drought and the extinction of species that benefit man. Global warming that is brought about by pollution, can lead to rising sea levels, and thus, flooding. At one time, all natural disasters were attributed to GOD's anger, and now, there is a scientific explanation for these calamities. However, if GOD is the master controller, he also controls the ecosystem, then these disasters can be said to be signs from HIM.*

Mike said, "I always get something new from you. You open my mind and broaden my horizons. You are truly my best friend, and I appreciate this." Susan was glad to hear this. She had the same feeling for him, and more. She was in love with him. However, she also valued him as her best friend, and she preferred to leave it at that.

Mike asked Susan what else happened while he was on vacation. She told him that she and her students went to the grand opening of a new art gallery, which she learned of on the TV news. She said that the paintings were absolutely unbelievable. They spent the entire day there, had a great time and came away with good feelings and emotions. She told him they were also able to speak with the artist. She was a beautiful woman, with a very interesting personality. They enjoyed talking to her as much as they enjoyed viewing the paintings. Susan recommended that Mike visit this gallery. He told her that he was very busy at the moment, composing new music and songs, but he was sure he would, when he had the time. She told him that she would like to talk to him, and get his reaction, after he went there. Then, they finished their espressos and went their separate ways.

When Mike returned to his apartment, he was overcome by the same vision of the girl, with the paintings flying behind her. He was so excited by this that he began to compose music and songs with every ounce of energy he had.

CHAPTER 40

After a lot of composing and writing music, Mike felt tired and wanted to relax a bit. He turned on the TV and the news was on. The story they were covering at the time had to do with the gallery. He was shocked to see the same painting from his vision in the gallery. He was more shocked when they focused on their interview with Nicole. She was the same girl from his vision! His state of shock left him with a bad feeling. He had a pain in his heart, trouble breathing, thinking or talking, and his hands were cold but sweaty. A while later he began to gain his composure. When he did, he knew that his life had changed, and it was now on a different level. His life was now going in a new direction.

He found the address of the gallery on the internet, and he planned to be there when it opened in the morning. He thought he might get lucky and meet the artist. Nevertheless, Mike had trouble falling asleep that night. His mind was preoccupied with thoughts of the gallery artist and how he might introduce himself to her. He didn't fall asleep until 3:00am, so he slept until the early afternoon. He woke up in a good mood though. He had the feeling that something very good was about to come into his life. It was as if his visions had led him to this. Like his brain had been reprogrammed by these visions to bring him to a magnificent climax.

Mike made a cup of coffee, as he usually did when he got out of bed, took a shower and then, called Max. He hadn't called Max for quite a while, because he was always busy. If he wasn't working for the band, he was busy working at home, which seemed like harder work than the music business. There was always so much to be done at home. To keep a clean home involves a lot of hard work, but it is necessary, and one always feels better when it's done. However, sometimes a person needs to relax and do nothing but nevertheless, most people feel guilty when they do nothing. They get the feeling that they are lazy and that makes them uncomfortable. They have the feeling that they should be doing something and getting something accomplished.

Mike was in luck. He caught Max at home. Max said, "How's it goin? It's been a long time since I've heard from you. I saw you at the pop music festival, but I haven't seen you since then because I've been very busy. I really enjoyed your music and songs. You've got a lot of talent, and I wish you the best of luck in your musical career."Mike smiled and thought that he should see more of Max in the future, because he really was a good friend. Mike mentioned that he saw a new gallery that had opened on the news, and asked Max if he wanted to get something to eat and go there after that. Max liked the idea, so Mike printed out the directions to the gallery on his computer.

After they ate, they drove to the gallery, which was open until 10:00pm, giving them plenty of time to walk around and view the paintings. Upon entering the gallery, they were confronted by a large painting with a multi-colored spiral, and two figures inside of it. Mike stood in front of the painting, staring and unable to move. The painting was like a magnet. It was like the painting was emitting energy. Just looking at it gave him a good feeling. It had a very strong effect on him. Max approached him and said, "Are you OK?" Mike slowly turned to look at Max and returned to reality. Max then said, "It really is a very good painting. I'd like to know who the artist is."

Mike told him, "All the paintings here were done by one woman. I saw a television interview with her on the news. That's why we're here." Max told Mike that it was a very interesting experience for him, and thanked him for bringing him here. They spent about three hours there, looking at one painting after another. They didn't just glance at them, but rather, they stood in front of each painting for a while.

Mike didn't get to meet Nicole, because she was usually there in the morning. Mike asked a worker when she was there and was told that she arrived when the gallery opened, and was usually there for about 3 hours. So, he and

Max left and drove back to the restaurant where they met. Max said, "I'll be happy to see you at one of my parties. Mike told Max that he missed his parties, and that he would give him a call. Max gave Mike five, and left. Mike went to his car, and went back to his apartment. There, he had a creative moment, and composed music until midnight.

CHAPTER 41

The next morning, Mike went back to the gallery. There were many people there, including members of the media. They surrounded Nicole, hoping for an interview, but Mike caught a glimpse of her. He thought to himself that this is the same girl that was in his visions. He never thought that his dream could come true, but now he believed it, because he saw her with his own two eyes. He just knew that she was his one true love. He could feel that she would be the one that he would spend the rest of his life with.

He was a bit apprehensive about meeting her, but he got a reprieve, because she was very busy and surrounded by others. He bided his time by walking around and viewing the paintings that were in his vision. Occasionally, he looked in Nicole's direction, waiting for her to have a moment alone, but he wasn't lucky this morning because she left with some journalists. So, Mike spent about another half hour there, and then went back to his apartment, where he had another creative moment, brought about by viewing the paintings that he also saw in his vision. This gave him satisfaction.

The next day, he got up early, to be at the gallery

when it opened, hoping to meet with the artist. However, the situation was the same as the day before. She was very busy with other people, and Mike didn't get a chance to meet her. This happened day after day. It became like going to work every morning. Nevertheless, every time he went, he discovered something new in the paintings, which gave him insight to compose new music and songs. The next morning Mike woke up with the feeling that he would meet that beautiful woman that day, and talk with her. He was a little bit nervous, and yet he was experiencing anticipation. The way one feels before something beautiful is going to happen.

When Mike arrived at the gallery, he met a journalist in the parking lot, who came to do an interview with Nicole. They had met previously at one of Max's parties. The man's name was Steve, and he recognized Mike. He said, "Hi, how are ya? I haven't seen you at Max's for quite a while. I saw you at the music festival though, and I liked you very much. You have a lot of talent, and I'm sure you'll go far." Mike thanked him and was encouraged by this. He told the journalist that he had seen Max a few days earlier, and he was sure that they would meet again at another one of his parties. Mike told Steve, the journalist, that he was a fan of Nicole's, and that he truly appreciated her work and would like to meet her and tell her how beautiful her paintings were. Steve told him that he could introduce them. He said that Nicole liked musicians, and that Mike would like to talk to her. Mike was ecstatic.

When they entered the gallery, Nicole was surrounded by journalists and other people. When they approached the group, they just listened to questions posed to her by the journalist who was conducting the interview at the time, and her answers. After she answered one of his questions, she turned around, and her attention was immediately grabbed by Mike, who was standing right in front of her. She just stared at him, and couldn't answer any more of the journalist's questions. She was in a state of shock. The journalist with whom she was doing the interview couldn't understand what was going on, but he knew that something interesting had happened. Everyone was looking in their direction, but they said nothing. Everything was quiet. It was like the calm before the storm. It was a waiting moment.

Steve used this moment to introduce them to each other. He said to Nicole, "My name is Steve. I'm a writer for the New York Times. I would like to ask you some questions, but before I do, I'd like to introduce you to my friend Mike, who is a well known composer and songwriter. Mike, meet Nicole, the artist, who created all these marvelous paintings. Mike has taken a great interest in your paintings and would like to talk to you about them." Nicole was still awestruck. She realized that Mike was the man from her dreams, and she also remembered him from the Pop festival. She enjoyed his music very much.

When she came back down to Earth, she smiled and

said, "It's very nice to meet the both of you."

Mike told Nicole how much he liked her paintings, and how they excited him. He said, "It's truly art. You are very talented, and have a great future ahead of you. Your name will be known worldwide. Thank you for sharing your gift with me."

Nicole appreciatively replied, "Thank you for your kind words. I remember you from the music festival. Thank you for sharing your gift with me. I really enjoyed your music and songs. You are also very talented." The eyes of both Mike and Nicole were bright and wet. When they both looked in each other's eyes, there was a very big connection between them. It was like love at first sight for each of them. It was what one sees in movies, paintings and reads about in poems. It was something that happened very rarely. It was like two halves meeting to make a whole. They could feel changes in their lives. It was an incredible feeling, and they knew that they would be seeing much more of each other. They just had a small conversation now, but they made arrangements to meet with each other at the gallery Saturday at 4:00pm. It was her day off, and they could talk much more. She told him that she wanted to walk him around the gallery, and was interested in getting his opinions of her paintings.

CHAPTER 42

Mike returned to his apartment, and Nicole stayed in the gallery for a while longer. However, everyone in the gallery had the feeling that something very important had happened between them. Mike returned to his apartment and felt very excited and creative. He began to compose music with Nicole on his mind. It was different now. He didn't have the vision anymore. He had met the real woman and she had taken his breath away. He was truly in love. He felt from his innermost being that she loved him too. He forgot all the women from his past and thought only of Nicole now. He was truly in love. It was like a dream come true.

When Nicole came back to her apartment she was very excited, happy and shaking. She couldn't believe what had happened. The man from her vision was a vision no longer. She had actually met him. She remembered the connection between them when they looked in each other's eyes. She just knew that she loved him, and he loved her. The feeling was absolutely wonderful. With Mike on her mind, she began painting pictures. She painted until midnight, when she had to sleep. She slept very soundly, like a newborn baby.

It was Saturday the beginning of the weekend, and it was her day off. She remembered she had made an arrangement to meet with Mike. At exactly 4:00 Mike was at the gallery, but Nicole was nowhere to be seen. He viewed pictures for an half hour. The door opened, and he saw Nicole. She was in a white suit, brown shirt and metallic brown high heeled shoes. She looked fantastic! Nicole just stood still, looking at Mike. He was in a grey suit, a black dress shirt and had a new haircut. He looked very clean and fresh. He looked great to Nicole. Mike, his heart racing, moved slowly towards Nicole. He moved closer and closer, until he was right in front of her. They just looked at each other for awhile, not saying a word. Mike realized that his heart no longer beat uncontrollably, and he had no worries. He felt so easy and comfortable to be with her, like he had known her all his life.

They started talking with each other, and they had a lot to talk about. Mike wanted to talk about his music and vision of Nicole and she wanted to talk about her painting and vision of him. Mike said to her, "I walked around a bit, saw some of your paintings, and I have to say that they really affect me. When I look at a painting, I get the feeling that I'm flying around, and at this moment, I see notes and thoughts of music fill my mind." Mike and Nicole walked around the whole gallery. They stopped in front of every painting, and Mike gave her his opinion. His opinions of each painting were exactly what message Nicole was trying to convey.

It was a mystery that the understanding between them ran so deep. At the same time, they both thought that they had to go home, and yet they both understood that they would be in love and together for the rest of their lives. When Mike returned to his apartment, he wanted to compose music and write songs. However, his feelings and emotions were different from when he had his vision of Nicole. Instead of visualizing her, he only thought about her now constantly. It was like she was there with him, and he felt truly happy. His life seemed so much clearer and brighter now. His life had transcended to a new level. He could now understand people who were in love and a person's feelings when his or her dream comes true. Nicole went back to her apartment feeling exactly as Mike did. She just felt like painting. They both worked through the night, and into the early morning, putting all their feelings, emotions and energy into music and painting. It was a truly creative time.

CHAPTER 43

The next morning, Mike woke up in a very good mood, with a lot of energy. He had a clear understanding of his new way in life and what he had to do. He saw his new life with Nicole and he liked what he saw. He called Nicole, and she picked up the telephone and said "Hi, Mike!" like she knew that he would call her at that particular moment. Nicole suddenly realized that it could have been anyone calling, but she felt that it would be him, and it was. She was happy to hear his voice. Mike asked her when they could see each other again, and they decided to meet Wednesday afternoon, around 3:00pm. Mike told her that time was good for him because he liked to go to bed later, and sleep until mid or late morning. He was surprised to hear that she also preferred to stay up late and sleep in. They were happy to find out that they had this in common. After the meeting time was set, they said, "I'll see you later," and went back to their normal routines.

Mike wanted to talk with someone about Nicole, just like anyone who is in love wants to talk about the subject. He immediately thought of Max, because he felt that Max was the only one he could talk to about this. He called Max, and he invited Mike to a party. He thought this was a great idea, since he hadn't been to one of Max's parties in quite a while. When he arrived, there good music was playing and the house was full of Max's friends, and friends of the friends. After wading through all the people, he finally found Max. They had a beer together, and Mike told him about meeting Nicole and his feelings about her. Max was both surprised and happy for Mike. Max told Mike that he would like to see her at one of his parties, and that everyone would enjoy seeing her and talking with her.

After the party, Mike returned to his apartment. For a moment he thought he would call Susan, but then he decided not to. He really didn't want to meet and talk with her, because his mind was totally on Nicole now. He didn't write or compose any music that night. All he wanted to do was think about Nicole and her painting's, relaxing and watching TV. He tuned in to the SciFi channel, which was showing his favorite program. When the program ended, he went to bed. While lying in bed, he thought of Nicole, the feelings between them, every moment they were able to spend together and how her eyes stayed directly on him during their conversations. He fell asleep with these good thoughts about her.

CHAPTER 44

It was a Monday, and Nicole had a very busy day at the gallery. There were many patrons, and Nicole met with Norman and Paul about a new project. They wanted to expand the gallery, but they needed more paintings. Nicole said that she had more in abstractionist style that she wanted to show to them. Larry, Aaron and Nicole went to Nicole's studio and took photos of them to put in the computer. They were just lines and spirals of different colors, but they were painted in such a way that energy emanated from them like fireworks. Larry asked Aaron to do more TV advertising. After they left her apartment, Nicole had the same feeling that Mike did. She wanted to talk to someone about him, because he was always on her mind. Paul had called her a few times, but she found any reason she could not to meet with him. She wanted to be with Mike, and she thanked God for giving him to her. She had to talk about this, so she decided to call Annette.

She wanted to talk to Annette about him because she felt that Annette was the only one she could talk to. When Nicole called, Annette was very happy to hear from her. This gave her the chance to get more news about Aaron. Annette told her that she was still dating him, and she liked him very much. She told Nicole that they had a good time together whenever they went out and great sex. However, their relationship did not seem to grow. Rather, it seemed to stay at the same level. Needless to say however, they were comfortable just hanging on to each other, not thinking about the future right now. She said that she thought she was in love with Aaron, and that she never had this kind of relationship with any other man she dated. It was a good feeling.

It turned out that Nicole and Annette both needed each other, to talk about Mike and Aaron respectively. Nicole told Annette about her feelings for Mike, and Annette listened with all her attention. She came to the conclusion that her relationship with Aaron was different from that between Nicole and Mike. While she and Aaron had a more friendly and balanced relationship, Nicole and Mike seemed to have some type of mystery love. It was something extraordinary.

CHAPTER 45

Mike called Nicole and asked her if she would like to go with him to a party at Max's house. She told him that she would, and that she looked forward to meeting some of his friends. When they met at Nicole's apartment, they forgot about everything. They both felt like they were the only ones in the world. They just wanted to be together, look on each other and tell each other about their innermost selves. After a while, they returned to reality and went to Max's house. There were many people in the house. Mike introduced Nicole to some of them and Max too. Max was shocked, and very happy to see Nicole there. Nicole had become quite the celebrity, since she was all the talk on the radio, newspapers and TV, and people couldn't help but hearing about her. The news that Nicole was there spread from one person to another until everyone knew. So, Max and a few of his close friends, Mike and Nicole gathered in a small group.

Soon, everybody at the party surrounded the small group, and began asking questions about Nicole's feelings and emotions, her likes and dislikes. Thus, the party atmosphere had changed. Now, the focus of attention had turned to Nicole. She had taken center stage. Mike was very proud and happy he had taken her with him. However, they weren't able to spend any time with each other. After the party, they both went to their own apartments, and went to bed thinking of each other.

The next morning, Mike woke up early, around 8:00am, and immediately wanted to call Nicole, but he realized that it was too early. To kill some time, he made a cup of coffee and read his email. By the time he had read his email and played a few games on the computer it was 10 o'clock and he couldn't wait any longer, and called Nicole. He was lucky to catch her still at home because she was just about to leave for a meeting at the gallery. Mike stated that since they weren't able to talk to each other at the party, he suggested they have dinner together, so that they could spend some time with each other. They met at 6:00pm at a restaurant called Bahama Breeze, and had a very good dinner. They still couldn't talk much though, because the restaurant was very busy and loud. Mike asked her if she would like to come to his apartment, and she said yes, but told him that she couldn't stay long, because she had to be at the gallery very early the next morning.

At Mike's apartment, he composed music and sang for Nicole. She was captivated by his music and song. Her heart began to beat faster, she began to quiver inside and her eyes began to tear up. She was deeply moved, and she felt nothing but love for him.

When Nicole went back to her apartment, she began to paint furiously. She got a lot of energy from Mike's music. It was an outstanding moment for her. She painted a picture of a tree, and on its branches were geometric shapes of different colors. Balls of different types, sizes and colors flew around the tree. It was a new style of painting for Nicole and, she liked it.

The next day, Mike called Nicole in the early afternoon, hoping she would be at home. He really wanted to hear her voice. When she answered the phone, he was so glad that she was already home from the gallery. She told him that she was free for the rest of the day, so they went for a walk in Central Park. They had a great conversation, and were very connected to nature, and their surroundings. When they were together, they were complete and happy. After strolling in the park, they went to a small café and had barbequed salmon and coffee. When they were ready to leave the café, Nicole asked Mike to come to her apartment.

When they entered Nicole's apartment, Mike noticed that it was very clean and cozy. There were beautiful flowers of different colors in vases, which had a good scent, but the best aroma of all was Nicole's perfume. Nicole asked Mike to come to her studio, so that she could show him her new painting of the tree. The new painting excited Mike, because of the amount of energy that it released. The energy came from the painting like waves, which Mike absorbed when they crashed into him. Mike had the desire to compose. He told Nicole that she had so much talent, and that meeting her was a gift from God.

Just being with Mike, made her want to paint. Mike watched Nicole as she started to paint, and incredible feelings and desires came upon him. He never felt this way before. While Nicole painted, he began to write music. Mike came closer to Nicole, and kissed her passionately. At this moment, they became like one and forgot who they were, and where they were. Then, Mike looked tenderly at Nicole and said, "I love you. I have the feeling that I've loved you all my life." Nicole was awestruck, because she had the exact same feelings and emotions. It was true love. It was the type of love one reads about in romance novels and poems. It was a mystery.

CHAPTER 46

It was fall, a very romantic time of the year. The leaves began to change color, the air seemed cleaner and it was a time for family festivities. At this time, a person thinks about one's past, present and future. About what happened in the past, about one's present situation and what could happen in the future. Analyzing the past and present, could help one see what the future might bring and thus, help him or her to take the correct steps accordingly. Everyone has a certain degree of faith, and vague thoughts of destiny. So, thought and correct actions can increase faith, and change one's destiny.

If something really bad were to happen to someone, support could soften the blow, and increase one's faith. Of course, if it is destiny, it would happen anyway, but faith and support make it easier to handle and perhaps, understand. Thus, if one engages in positive thinking and imagination, prayer and meditation, one could change a negative situation into something more positive. For example, if one were to be in auto accident, a fatality could be reduced to a minor injury, with proper thought and action. A person cannot know what awaits him, but with the right way of living and proper action, adverse effects can be minimized.

Therefore, one should always smile at every creature, and always try to give help and forgiveness. Always give support and loyalty to everyone, and only good things will come to you. Do not express negative thoughts and words about anyone or anything, because you will be emitting negative energy, and that is what you will receive. If something bad were to happen to you, just be grateful that it was not something worse, something really terrible.

The fall season had an effect on Mike too. Often he would get caught up thinking about his past, present and future. All kinds of thoughts would run through his head, and he would stop on one after another, analyzing them. He believed that he was very lucky in this life. Everything good seemed to be going his way, and he was especially fortunate to have met Nicole. She was a wonderful person. It was when Mike was thinking about her that she called. Mike was both surprised and happy to hear from her. She never called him before, he always called her. Nicole told Mike that she had some free time, and wanted to see him. He was always on her mind. Nicole was truly attracted to him. Some men don't like women to call them. They prefer to call the women when the notion strikes them. It gives them a sense of freedom but, if it's true love, men don't think this way. Nicole felt that Mike would like her call. They are just happy to hear the voice of the one he or she loves. To them, it does not matter who calls who, because they are just in love. Mike invited Nicole to his apartment, and said, "I'll be there in about half an hour."

When Mike opened the door, he was glad to see Nicole. She was like a breath of fresh air. They looked at each other, smiled and kissed. There was no awkwardness between them, like the barrier that can exist between a man and woman when they meet. Mike and Nicole were not afraid to say or do whatever came naturally unlike many who try to be something they're not, in order to impress the other. We can't always live up to other's expectations. This type of behavior will ultimately backfire, and never lead to love. So, it is better to be the real you, and not care what others may think. This will lead to long term love. Just try not to be antisocial.

Mike asked Nicole, "Would you like something to drink? How about something to eat?" Nicole answered, "I'll have white wine if you have it, and I am a bit hungry." Mike said, "I've got the wine, and I'll make something to eat." He made chicken cordon bleu and caesars salad. He set the table like a waiter at a fine restaurant. The table cloth was white, the glasses were tall and red and the plates were red with gold edging. On the table was a vase of beautiful flowers, a bottle of fine white wine and candles in brass holders. Everything looked traditional and classy. Nicole was shockingly surprised.

Mike asked Nicole to sit down, and with a smile and

love in her eyes, sat down on the chair while Mike moved it to the table. Mike was a true gentleman, and he had very good manners. They began their dinner with appetizers of wine and cheese. Afterward, Mike served the main entree of chicken and salad. Nicole noticed three aspects of Mike's character that she had not seen before: he was well mannered, he had good taste and he was a great cook. It was the best dinner that they'd ever had. The excellent food, great design and wonderful companionship, displayed their love for each other. They felt blessed.

CHAPTER 47

Mike asked Nicole if she would dance with him, and she readily accepted. He put on some slow, romantic music by Frank Sinatra, and as they danced, they held each other very tight. They felt like they were the only ones in the world, and nothing else mattered to them. The only thing that was important to them at this moment was each other. Their eyes were closed, and they heard only music, and saw one painting after another. They both shared the same vision. It was like two halves coming together to make one whole.

Mike spoke tender words to Nicole. She was very sensitive, and his words really touched her. She exploded with emotions and feelings, and became very hot and full of energy. They held and kissed each other all over. Their kisses were like water in a stream. They were gentle and hard, faster and slower, longer and shorter. This was a moment of true love. They forgot about everything else, but their feelings for each other. They just melted together and became one. They were so relaxed with each other, that they couldn't move or talk. They were so sensitive to each other, that it was as if they were afraid of destroying this moment and returning to reality. With their eyes closed, they held each other and became one with the universe. When Mike and Nicole finally did come back to reality, they looked in each other's eyes, and it was exactly the same as when their eyes first met. They knew this was meant to be.

The next morning, Mike made coffee and a light breakfast for both of them. Nicole called Norman afterward, and told him that she needed a week off, and that she would see them all after one week. They wanted to spend one week together. Then, they went to Central Park, where they could enjoy the open space, clean air and fall colors. It had become their favorite place to walk around, and talk about anything that came to mind. Sometimes, they didn't say anything to each other. This didn't leave them feeling awkward or empty because, there was harmony between them and nature.

CHAPTER 48

When they returned to Mike's apartment, Mike told Nicole that he had a truly creative moment after watching her paint in her studio. She told him that the same thing happened to her after she listened to his music and songs. Mike made the suggestion that they both have one studio, where he could compose while she painted, and she could paint while he composed. Nicole told him that she thought it was a great idea, so they went to Nicole's apartment, packed everything, and moved to Mike's apartment. They wanted to spend as much time together as they could.

They spent the entire day getting the studio organized for the both of them. After a long day, everything was finally done. All things were in their proper place, and they felt they had accomplished something very important to them. They found each other. Their vision and dream had come true and their lives were now complete. Now that all the work of moving and organizing was done, it left them very tired and they fell asleep. When they woke up the next morning, they looked at each other, smiled and kissed, and went to the kitchen to make coffee and breakfast. They knew that they would spend the rest of their lives together.

After coffee and breakfast, they went to their shared studio where they could create together. Mike began to compose music, which prompted Nicole to start painting. Her painting gave him energy and emotions to compose more. However, when Mike stopped composing, Nicole immediately stopped painting. She realized that she couldn't paint without hearing Mike's music. Usually, she painted whenever she had the vision of a man with blue eyes accompanied by sounds of music. But, she didn't have that vision anymore. It had become reality. She now knew that she depended on his music. At the same time, Mike couldn't compose anymore, and he realized that he depended on seeing Nicole paint to create music. At this point, they both looked at each other lovingly. Mike came to Nicole, kissed her and held her. They both came to the realization that they were the common denominator in their creativity. They felt their love for each other would last until death. It was truly love through art.

.

8391412R1

Made in the USA
Charleston, SC
05 June 2011